Better Than Running at Night

3/36373

Better Than Running at Night

Hillary Frank

Houghton Mifflin Company

Boston 2002

In memory of Morse Hamilton, my teacher and friend

www.houghtonmifflinbooks.com

The text of this book is set in Scala.

Library of Congress Cataloging-in-Publication Data
Frank, Hillary.
Better than running at night / Hillary Frank.
p. cm.
Summary: A freshman art student from Manhattan spends her first year away from home in New England.
ISBN 0-618-25073-5 (pbk.) ISBN 0-618-10439-9 (hardcover)
[1. Art schools—Fiction. 2. Universities and colleges—Fiction. 3. Interpersonal relations—Fiction.
4. Sex—Fiction.] I. Title.
PZ7.F8493 Be 2005   [Fic]—dc21   2002000218

Manufactured in the United States of America
HAD 10 9 8 7 6 5 4 3 2 1

Acknowledgments

I am grateful to the following people for taking me seriously when I was a teenager. Without their support this book wouldn't exist.

Leona, Dick, and Josh Frank
Karl Decker
Arlene Skutch
Morse Hamilton
Jonathan Strong
Jay Cantor
Mary Brigid Barrett

Thanks also to the faculty at the New York Academy of Art for teaching me how to draw. And to David Jamieson for always answering the question "What do you think of this?"

Huge thanks to Eden Edwards for seeing a novel in a twenty-page story and for being such an open-minded and insightful editor.

Threesome

I wanted to move freely: swing my arms and jump around. But the Devil wouldn't stop dirty dancing with me. He grinned through glistening red face paint, grinding his hips against my body. The attention was nice, but my thigh got stuck in his crotch for too long.

Finally he spun me out right at the beginning of "Love Me." When I turned around, I was facing a sneering Elvis with a microphone. It was one of those black mikes with an orange Nerf ball on top that you use when you're an eight-year-old living-room rock star. Elvis approached me, singing sincerely with hand gestures and all, as if he'd been waiting for this opportunity all night. Like he'd requested it. Before he got close enough to fully serenade me, the Devil pulled me back toward him, grinding slowly from behind. He spun me around so I was facing him and lifted me, twirling me in the air, making my gypsy skirts catch wind.

"Looks like I picked up the cutest girl at this party," he said, directly in my ear since the music was deafeningly loud.

Elvis circled around with us, lip-synching in my direction and making puppy-dog eye contact whenever possible.

The Devil put me back on the ground, which Elvis interpreted

1

as an invitation to cut in. Soon the three of us were dancing together; suggestive movements, since the Devil would have it no other way, and Elvis clutching his microphone. By the end of the song, Elvis had placed his mike in the back pocket of his leather pants, so our faces were much closer. Elvis fumbled with one of the strands of beads around my neck and kissed me — first little pecks, then longer and slower. The Devil's fingers crept up a different strand, tugging as they went. His hand bumped into Elvis's and Elvis stopped kissing me to push the Devil's hand away. The Devil quickly wrapped his arm around my waist and whisked me away and kissed me, too. Between kisses he bit my lips gently.

I'd never thought of biting as a good thing before.

When Elvis started stroking my hair, the Devil turned and kissed him hard on the lips, as if that would distract him from me. But it didn't seem to faze him. Elvis went along with the kisses, then broke away and grabbed me again. Soon we were all making out, taking turns with who got control. I could tell who was who without opening my eyes; the Devil kept trying new things like sucking my lips and blowing air into my mouth, while Elvis always had the same average French kiss.

Elvis's lips and chin were smeared with red makeup. Some from the Devil's face, some from my lipstick. The Devil's face paint was all splotchy, with bits of flesh showing through, especially around his mouth.

The more we made out, the more I realized this guy didn't look like Elvis at all. It wasn't anything specific, but he definitely was not Elvis. He began to lose his charm and I gravitated toward the Devil.

We both stopped giving Elvis his turn, so eventually he sauntered off. I was still smooching the Devil at the end of the last song, and he offered to walk me home.

We left under the glowing exit sign.

Tea with the Devil

He held my hand and tried to warm it, squeezing my fingers between his own.

I wondered if the Devil had ever held hands with a gypsy before. Or with any person, for that matter. I thought his fiery hand would scorch my fingers off, but out there in the frosty night, it wasn't doing me much good.

I didn't have tights on and the chilled air danced around my legs. My teeth chattered.

"Cold?" he asked.

"Good guess," I said, shivering.

He put his arm around me. "Where's your place?"

"Number 301." I pointed down Artist's Row. "Kind of a hike."

"We're practically neighbors!" He squeezed me against his side. "I've got a better idea! Come to my place for tea. It's on your way, and you'll warm up faster. What could be hotter than the Devil's lair, anyway?" He winked.

"Nothing I can think of." I pressed up against him for warmth.

3

He lived in a small brick house that was set back from the sidewalk by a sparsely wooded area. We followed a path through the leafless trees, saying nothing as we walked, my beads clanking and skirts rustling. There were three studio apartments in the building. We got to his through the side door.

Inside, his steamy radiator banged and hissed. He was right; it couldn't have been much hotter without being a sauna.

I made my way through the sculptures of fire hydrants and fire hydrant parts that cluttered his floor. The floorboards were stained a slightly lighter brown than the wood paneling that covered the walls. The ceiling light radiated a dim yellow glow that didn't quite reach the outer limits of the room.

The bang of the radiator sounded like little guys with hammers were running up and down the pipes.

Since the frameless futon mattress was the only place to sit, I sat on it. As he went to the kitchen to boil water, I said, "I'm Ellie, by the way."

"Oh, I'm Satan," he said, walking back to shake my hand. "Nice to meet you. No, just kidding. Name's Nate. Nate Finerman. As in: You Never Met a . . ."

His eyebrows arched outward as he smiled. Removing his horns and thin red hood, he revealed a head of dark thick hair that radiated around his scalp as if he'd rubbed a balloon on it. I'd never seen anything like it.

He noticed me staring at his hair and said, "Like my 'do? It's been growing straight out like this ever since I shaved it. I want to see how long it'll get before it falls normally again."

His teapot was like the one my parents have at home: the kind that whistles.

The refrigerator buzzed.

Down at futon level, some of the fire hydrant sculptures stood taller than me. The biggest ones were constructed with foam core and cardboard, and the smallest were in clay. The wall by his bed was plastered in pictures of him with various stylish women. Above those snapshots was a neat row of pages from magazines like *Cosmo*. None of the ladies were naked, but their clothes said that could be changed very quickly.

On the night table was one framed photograph, of a man wearing glasses, carrying a bag of golf clubs.

After he'd filled the kettle, Nate returned to sit with me. He put his arm around me and ran his fingertips against my scalp. I rubbed his cheek with my thumb, trying to smudge the red face paint back to an area where it had been displaced in a reverse lipstick mark. I laughed.

"What's funny?" he asked, pressing his fingers harder against my scalp.

"Nothing." I took a deep breath to regain composure. I didn't want him to know I was laughing because the last time I'd kissed someone was at a middle school spin-the-bottle party. Only in my dreams did someone make out with a loner like me. And I'd never imagined two guys would want me at the same time.

Two guys. I couldn't let that happen again.

The radiator shhhhed like an annoying librarian.

Nate brought my face toward his and started kissing me. He

5

kissed in a hurry like it was make-out rush hour. I withdrew to look at him.

"What's wrong?" he asked.

"Nothing."

He looked into my eyes as if he was hunting for something he lost.

I glanced over his shoulder at the red digits on his alarm clock. It was already several hours into tomorrow.

He slowly pushed me down so I was lying on my back, and draped one of his legs across my middle.

I stared at the cobweb in the corner of the ceiling.

"You're not ready," he said, almost accusingly.

"For what?"

He laughed. "You'd better go home before something happens."

He rolled off me. I sat up.

"Did I do something wrong?" I asked.

"No." He stroked my face. "The problem is, you're doing everything *right*. I don't want to ruin it."

More banging from the radiator.

He helped me get my coat on and dragged the zipper up at inchworm pace. When he reached my chest, he pulled it back down — so slowly, I heard the zipper hit each bump. He paused to look me in the eye, then zipped me all the way up.

"It's better this way," he said.

"I guess."

"Don't be insulted." He hugged me.

"Well, Happy New Year," I said, even though technically New Year's Eve had been two nights ago.

"Yeah, you too," he sighed.

I turned toward the door.

"Wait," he said, "I was going to walk you home."

"It's okay," I said. "It's only a few blocks."

"You sure?"

"Yes."

"Well can I at least come and visit sometime?"

"Sure, stop by if you want."

"You said 301, right?"

"Right. Big white place. One-F on the buzzer. But if you forget, knock on my window. Front right corner."

"You really should let me walk you home."

"I told you, I'll be okay," I said. "I'm from Manhattan. What're you so worried about anyway?"

He tucked my hair behind my ears. "You never know who's out there waiting for a looker like you."

Running at Night

I guess it was best that I left Nate's house. I didn't know anything about him except that he dressed like the Devil and lived down the street. The cold air stung my face, so I ran. I couldn't put my gloves on because there was melted lollipop goo stuck to the fuzz. I'm always forgetting things in my pockets.

Clanking and rustling as I ran, I inhaled the cold. I ran faster and faster, swallowing mouthfuls of the tingling air.

My boots clomped along the pavement and my shadow grew and shrank and grew again as I passed street lamps. There was nobody else out, so I zigzagged from curb to curb, crossing the double yellow lines. Doing this back home would've been a death wish; drivers own the sleepless streets there. But here, the road was all mine.

When I was running, the wintry air didn't hurt my skin; it made my entire body feel fresh and alive. I sprinted past my apartment, to the end of the block. I made a U-turn at the stop sign and thought, "It doesn't get better than this."

I stopped, out of breath, at my building. It was an old mansion that used to be an insane asylum. Now it was full of college students.

I walked up the three thin wide steps and through the front door to the empty hardwood hallway. If anyone else was up, I couldn't hear them.

A pile of balled-up packing tape and Styrofoam peanuts welcomed me home. Boxes of books and bags of clothes were scattered around the living room. The bathroom and kitchen were all set up, though. My parents had seen to that.

In the bathroom mirror, my face was all smudgy with gypsy and Devil makeup. It took a while to wash it off. I had gotten used to no makeup at all since I'd removed it from my daily routine. I'd forgotten what a pain it was.

I tossed my costume on the floor in a heap and got into my pajamas.

I shut my eyes. There was nothing I wanted more than sleep.

Enveloped in my blankets, I wondered what would be happening at that moment if I hadn't left Nate's. Maybe we'd be drinking tea.

The glow-in-the-dark stars above met my sudden wide-eyed stare.

The kettle had never whistled.

The Stuff

The phone was ringing. It took me a minute to realize it wasn't a fire alarm. Nine A.M. Had to be a relative.

"Have you got the stuff?" asked a scratchy voice.

"What stuff?" I bolted upright. "Who is this?"

"It's me," he said, switching to his regular voice. "Who'd you think it was? Your other dad?" He laughed.

I didn't.

"Well anyway, how's life at Nekked?"

"It's NECAD, Dad. N-E-C-A-D. As in New England College of Art and Design. How many times do I have to tell you?"

"Might as well be Nekked, with all those *naked* people running around!" he said with a laugh.

"Oh yeah, there's just *swarms* of them running through the

streets, Dad. You'd think it was a nudist marathon." Sometimes I have trouble controlling my sarcasm.

"Maybe I should give you to your mother."

"Maybe." I tried to say it as straight as possible.

As he handed her the receiver, I heard a muffled "She'd rather speak to you." I rolled my eyes even though he wasn't there to see.

"Hey, El!"

"Hi Mom."

"Is everything okay?"

"Yeah, yeah, everything's fine," I said. "Dad's just getting on my nerves. You know, his usual jokes."

"You could ask him to stop."

"I try. It's no use."

"Well, we didn't call to get you down. Are you settling in all right?"

"Yeah."

"Did you go to the Artist's Ball?"

"Yeah. Last night."

"Any cool costumes?"

"Some. One guy wore a chain mail suit. He made it himself."

"Wow. Did you have a good time?"

"It was pretty fun."

"Make any friends?"

"Kind of."

"*Kind of?*"

Well, Mom, you wouldn't believe it, but I made out with the Devil.

"It's hard to meet people when the music's so loud you can hear it pounding in your head the next morning," I said.

"Right," she said. "Well, you'll meet people soon. This is a really exciting time for you. I bet there are lots of cute guys, too!"

"Why do you care so much about me making friends and meeting guys?"

"Oh, El," she sighed. "I just want you to be happier than you were in high school. It's nice to have friends. And to have boyfriends."

"I'll be okay."

In the background I heard Dad say, "Has she finished unpacking?"

"Tell him not completely," I said.

"I felt bad leaving without getting your place in order," she said.

"It's fine," I said. "You did more than you had to. I can take care of it."

"I know you can," she said. "But it's your first time on your own. If Dad didn't have to get back to prepare for trial, I would've stuck around till you were settled in."

"She'll be fine, Marsha!" Dad said. "Just tell her to make sure she unpacks soon!"

"Did you hear that?" Mom asked.

"Yes," I groaned. "Why does he care so much?"

"Your father is an obsessively tidy person," she said. "It drives him crazy to think that somewhere in another state, his daughter might have clothes strewn across the floor."

"No, I just want to know if she's unpacked. That's it," he said loud enough for me to hear.

"Okay, Len," she humored him.

"Why don't you let your mother talk?" I heard him say to her. "She's been waiting patiently."

"Grandma's over?" I asked.

"She's right beside me," she said. "I'll pass you over to her. Good luck in class on Monday. Call if you need anything. And don't forget to notify your father when you've unpacked!"

"Tell him not to worry," I said. "I'll hire a skywriter to write a message over the city: ELLIE'S UNPACKED."

"I'm sure he'll appreciate it," she said. "Love you."

"Love you, too."

She passed off the phone.

"Hello?" Grandma always answered the phone like she was making a guess to solve a riddle.

"Hi, Grandma," I said, lying back down. "How are you?"

"I'm well," she said. "But more important is how are you? The new place, the new peoples." Sometimes Grandma messed up her English. Mom said she did it on purpose because it sounded good with her German accent.

"I'm fine," I said. "I wore your skirts and beads last night."

"Your mother tells me you went to be a gypsy at the party."

"That's right," I said. A long sunny rectangle warmed my face through black bars over my window. All the first-floor apartments had them, to protect us from criminals.

"Is a good thing I gave you those old clothes," she said. "They were crowded in my closet, and I would have taken them to the Goodwill."

"Glad I could save you the trip."

She laughed. "And is there a young man in your life?"

"Oh, not really."

"No? An adorable girl like you?"

"I'm not in a big hurry."

What did she want from me? I hadn't even been here a week yet. Grandma must've been fast back in the day.

"I don't want to be keeping you long," she said.

"I like talking to you."

"Well, we're getting going for brunch."

"Okay," I said. "Thanks for the clothes."

"You're welcome," she said. "Good luck and good-bye." She made a kissing noise.

I kissed back. "Bye Grandma. Have fun at brunch."

I hung up the phone and fell back to sleep hugging my pillow.

The sun's elongated shadow lines crept across my bed.

Most Individual

A rapping on the window made my heart jump. Nate's face grinned through the bars. I leapt out of bed.

"Not up yet?" he yelled. His face was faint. Only the high points of his nose, cheeks, and chin were illuminated by a light on the side of my building.

"I didn't leave your place until three in the morning!" I yelled back. "*And* I had trouble sleeping!"

"Well rise and shine and let me in!"

He was right. I should've been up. It was four o'clock.

When I got to the door he was already there, leaning on the door frame as if he'd been waiting for hours. His face, no longer red and shiny, was gentler than I'd expected. His features were angular, but they looked like they'd be soft to touch. I had an urge to run my fingers through his staticky looking hair.

A huge scar began under his chin and ran along the base of his jaw.

"So this is where I live," I said as he entered.

I was hungry and didn't feel like making small talk.

He looked around, surveying the scene. "Just moved?"

"Yeah."

He walked over to the kitchen. "Hey, champagne!" he said, lifting the bottle from the counter. "We'll have to celebrate sometime!"

"Okay," I said. "I'm saving it for a special occasion."

"That's cool," he said, putting the bottle down. "What do you want to do tonight?"

"*Tonight?*"

"What, you're sick of me already?"

"No," I said. "I just didn't know we had plans. I've got to get ready if we're going out." I pointed at my pajamas.

"Who needs plans?" He grinned. "We can make it a night in."

"*Well*, okay," I said. "But I still have to shower. If you want to stay, you can."

"I think I will." He jumped backward and landed butt-first on my bed. The mattress springs squeaked.

In the shower I remembered how he'd said "You're not ready," and I didn't need a mirror to know the color was rushing to my cheeks like a shark to a flesh wound.

I turned the temperature to cold for a three-second jolt before shutting the water off and dressing in the bathroom. I heard my Soundgarden CD, *Superunknown,* blasting in the bedroom.

When I came out, Nate lowered the volume. My high school yearbook was in his lap.

"I hope you don't mind me looking at this," he said. "It was at the top of this box. I couldn't resist."

"It's all right," I said, turning down the music even more. "What've you found?"

I sat beside him on the bed. My hair cooled my head and dripped on my shoulders, leaving wet spots on my shirt.

"Well, I think I found you," he said. "Yelinsky, right?"

"Right."

"Except it looks nothing like you. What's with all the black? And the cropped hair? And the makeup? It looks like a clown painted your face at a funeral."

"*Thanks.*"

"No, I mean you look so much better now. Whoa! Is that a tear penciled in at the corner of your eye?"

"Yes," I said. "It took me a long time to perfect that look."

Nate nodded his head along with the repeating bass riff on the CD. "I would think so," he said, flipping the pages. He stopped to look at the Superlatives page. "Hey, that's you!" He pointed at the picture labeled Most Individual. "You must've been popular."

"Not at all," I said. "I think they chose me because of my paintings and my style. I was always the first in my grade to discover the latest."

"Like what?" he asked, brushing a few strands of hair out of my face.

"Like dyeing my hair blue-black. And shaving the lower half of my scalp. Like thermal underwear beneath T-shirts. Safety-pinned patch pants."

"That doesn't sound *so* crazy," he said. "Aren't you from New York?"

"Yeah, I didn't stand out in the city, but my school was pretty preppie."

"So where are your piercings?"

"Don't have any," I said. "I guess I have a low threshold for pain. But mostly I can't stand talking to people with spikes and hoops sticking out of their face — it's so distracting. I always want to tell them to brush it away, like it's some leftover piece of food."

He laughed. "You really *are* Most Individual, aren't you?"

On the Floor at McDonald's

That night I'd been planning on cooking a real meal with a little of each food group, since my fridge was stocked with ingredients for the quick and easy dishes my mom had taught me before I left. But sleeping all day had killed my motivation. My droopy muscles begged me to take them back to bed. So I only made it through the pasta group, which we ate directly out of the pot. And thanks to Nate and his fake ID, we also covered the alcohol group. Carlo Rossi Burgundy, one of those huge jugs.

Nate filled two water glasses practically to the top with wine. "Who needs wineglasses?"

We sat on my living room floor, leaned up against a couple of book boxes, pasta pot between us.

"Are you a freshman?" I asked.

"Nope, sophomore," he said. "I transferred from the Art Institute — you know, the one in San Francisco. Started here last semester. How 'bout you? I don't remember seeing you before last night."

"Freshman," I said. "I haven't even started yet. I was deferred."

"Oh, so you're new!" he said. "That's good. I wouldn't want to think I'd overlooked such a cutie."

He poured us both more wine. I hadn't finished my first glass yet.

I fidgeted with my fork.

"You need some wall decorations," Nate said. "Empty white walls make me nervous."

"Yeah, you have lots of pictures up, don't you."

"Gotta have stuff to look at."

I plucked at my fork prongs.

"So who was the guy in the picture on your night table?" I

asked, even though what I really wanted to ask was, Who were those girls on your wall?

"That's the last picture taken of my dad." All giddiness dropped from his face and I was afraid to ask my next question.

"You mean last picture because . . ." I began.

Nate closed his eyes. "Because he died," he said quietly.

"I'm sorry," I said. "You don't have to talk about it if you don't want."

"It's okay." He opened his eyes and turned to look at me. "It was a long time ago."

"How old were you?"

"Almost two. So I don't remember him. Sometimes I think I do, but really my memories are all from photographs."

"Maybe you don't want to answer this," I said, "but how did he die?"

"We were out sneaker shopping," he said. "Me, my dad, and my two sisters. He had taken us into McDonald's for lunch."

I dropped my fork and it clanged against the side of the pot.

"He had a heart attack. Collapsed dead right then and there, on the floor at McDonald's. He was holding me and when he fell his arms were still wrapped around my body."

"Wow," I said. "I'll never think of McDonald's the same way again."

"Neither did I," he said. "I won't set foot in any fast-food places."

"That's awful," I said. "To have something so traumatic happen when you were so young."

"I never knew who my dad was," he said. "And I never will."

He wrinkled his forehead as he talked about it. There were two deep creases between his eyebrows. I told him I wanted to get into his head, to smooth the grooves from the inside. He told me that was possibly the sweetest thing anyone had ever said to him.

I'm not somebody who's often described as "sweet."

He swigged the rest of his wine, then poured himself another glass and gave me what he called a "warm up."

I retrieved my fork from the pot. Sauce got all over my hand. I licked it off.

Nate was smiling at me.

"What?" I asked.

"Nothing." He shook his head.

"Come on, tell me."

"It's just . . . you looked really cute cleaning the sauce off your hand."

"Thanks, I think," I said. "I don't really know what to say to that."

"You don't have to say anything."

"Are you done?" I pointed at the spaghetti mound in the bottom of the pot.

"Couldn't be more done!" He patted his belly. It made a hollow popping sound.

I got up to bring the pot and forks to the sink, but he stood and pushed me back down by my shoulders. "No, allow me," he said.

The wine had made me sleepy. I brought my glass to my bed. Walking made me lightheaded. Seated on the floor, I hadn't noticed that I was getting drunk.

The sink splashed and the pot bonged each time it hit the faucet.

When Nate finished washing, he flipped off all the lights except my bedside lamp. I had finished my wine and was lying on my side. He lay down, mirroring my position.

His hand ran over my face a few times from top to bottom. Then he kissed the tip of my nose. He dragged his fingers in tiny circles on my neck.

Goosebumps rose on that side of my body.

Nate reached behind him and switched off the lamp.

Before my eyes adjusted to the dark, he was like an invisible phantom stroking my skin.

I massaged his scalp beneath fistfuls of hair and our faces got closer. He put his cheek against mine. Then he moved his face lower so his forehead was in my eye socket. And his eye socket cradled my cheek. My zygoma.

"This fits," he said.

He was right; it felt like our faces were meant to be attached in precisely this manner.

I couldn't get his father's death out of my mind.

In my drunken state, Nate's pain seemed tangible, like I might be able to actually rub it out of his skin into a ball and throw it through the window. It would be easy; the window was just above my head.

But heavy sleep made my fingers forget, and my hand fell on his chest.

A little later, when it was still dark, I woke up remembering that I had been on a mission. Both his hands were clasping mine. I don't think I moved, but he must've sensed that I was awake because he started whispering to me.

"I dig you, Ellie Yelinsky," he said, so softly I barely heard it.

I nodded.

"I dig you too, Nate Finerman," I said back to him. I had never used the word *dig* like that.

I was tempted to write down what we talked about because I knew I'd forget everything in the morning except his lips moving against my ear.

He squeezed my hand against his chest so hard I could feel his heart pounding, like it wanted out.

I wished we could've stayed like that forever: on the border of sleep and sunrise, not quite making sense and a little dizzy.

But it would've been awkward if I had stopped him from putting the moves on me.

Regular

"Do you want any coffee?" I asked him the next day.

He was sitting on the edge of my bed, holding his head. His hair was flat on one side.

"Please. Regular." He nodded his head without raising it and left it heavy in his palms, pushing his elbows into his thighs.

When the coffeemaker let out its last gurgles, I went to the kitchen. From the bed, Nate watched me through the doorway. I was about to pour cream in his cup, when his head jolted and he asked, "What are you doing!" as if I had dumped the coffee all over his face. "I said reg-u-lar."

"Exactly," I said, "cream and sugar."

"Don't you get it? Regular: nothing in it."

"In New York, regular means cream and sugar. If you want it black, just say so."

"Of course I do. None of that sweet stuff."

I apologized. I didn't feel like fighting both him and my hangover.

"That's all right," he said, laying his head back in his hands.

Unpacked

"Did I *unpack!*" I screamed into the receiver as soon as he picked up. I had meant to sound more reserved than that.

"You found it," he said calmly.

"What's this supposed to *mean?*"

"First: relax."

"I *am* relaxed," I said between clenched teeth.

"I just want you to try it," he said. "Try it with some new friends."

"But I don't *want* to. I'm throwing it out. Right now. It's in the garbage." I held the receiver over the wastebasket so he could hear my foot slam the pedal on the metal trash can. The baggie crinkled when it dropped.

"Great idea," he said. "Now, if the cops find it in your trash, it'll have your fingerprints all over it."

I snatched it out. "I have another idea."

"So do I," he said. "Smoke it."

I got an empty jar from my painting supplies box. It was meant for turpentine. "I'm emptying the contents of this bag into a jar," I said. "And I'm putting the jar on my spice rack." I placed it next to the oregano.

"How will you label it?"

"Poison. Do Not Use." I found a Sharpie and drew a skull and crossbones on the glass.

"Will you at least drink the champagne I gave you when you got your acceptance letter?"

"I'm saving it."

"Listen, if you don't get this out of your system now," he said, "imagine what you'll be like when you're forty."

"I can just see it," I said. "I'll be a sober, lively woman. And everyone will say, What a shame she turned out that way."

"Look," he said. "These things happen at one time or another. It's better to try it now with the rest of the kids than to end up a lone junkie. You're a girl who likes to keep to herself. I'm not saying that's a bad thing, but those morbid paintings you make, and those pictures of skinned cadavers you love have me worried. And not that I liked that morose look, but you're dressing all normal now. You're trying to grow up too soon. You need some sort of release."

"Art *is* my release."

"Ellie, everyone experiments with danger at some point, and

the way I see it, the most harmless way to do it is at an early age. That way you outgrow it before it's too late."

"I'll find my own way of having fun, Dad."

"That," he said, "is exactly what I'm afraid of."

Some Good Dope

Ever since I graduated from high school, my dad kept telling me he could hook me up with some good dope. I never thought he'd actually follow through.

He never understood that I didn't get my thrills out of getting high; I got my kicks from oil paint. And not from sniffing it, just using it.

I was always painting screaming heads strangled by boa constrictors, mangled bodies pinned to bleeding walls by arrows through the heart, vultures devouring the brains out of lost souls on scorching sand.

During free periods, while other kids hung out in the cafeteria or did homework in the library, I would set up a canvas and painting supplies in an empty art room. Teachers would poke their heads in, and when they saw what I was up to they would back away slowly, as if any sudden movements would cause my picture to attack. "Why don't you ever paint anything *nice*?" they'd ask.

"Because," I'd tell them, evoking an evil smile, "I don't *think* anything nice."

But when my peers came by, they were full of compliments, full of awe. "You have the best ideas," they'd say. "It's like you can see our souls." That's exactly how I wanted them to think of me: as a painter for our generation, as a teenage soul psychic.

Once school ended, I painted at home. My dad would ask questions like, "Why a vampire?" and "Do people's faces really turn that green when they're dead?" I got sick of telling him I had artistic license to paint whatever I wanted, and that I exaggerated on purpose to heighten the sense of pain in the picture.

I started to avoid these confrontations by spending time looking at art by other people — something I hadn't done much before. I'd go to the Met and stay there for hours, copying paintings with a pencil into my sketchbook. One painting I always went back to was of a beheaded martyred saint. His head lay beside his body and a thin stream of blood spouted from his neck. This depiction of death was a little too conservative for me, but still it was fun to copy.

Christ's Descent into Hell was more to my taste. It was painted by an unknown artist, in the style of Hieronymus Bosch, and was full of fiery scenes. This painting took me the longest to draw because of all the figures and hellish details.

One day, I thought, I'll paint an image of hell so horrifying, people will feel tortured just looking at it.

Ivan the Terrible

When I wasn't in the museum, I'd be at the library, copying Leonardo's drawings of cadavers. I wished I could understand his writing, but it was all in Italian and backwards. Leonardo's dead people looked so — well, dead. If only I could learn to draw like that, I thought, my paintings would be more powerful; I could show real emotion, real agony, real fear. Somehow, I needed to get practice painting realistically.

In the library I came across Ilya Repin's *Ivan the Terrible and His Son Ivan*. A portrayal of the Russian tyrant cradling his son and only heir after having murdered him. The gory picture was said to have made ladies faint.

But it wasn't the amount of blood gushing from the young Ivan's head wound or his father's fingers' inability to stop the leakage that frightened me. It was those eyes. The look on Ivan's face that said, "Holy shit, I just did something that can't be changed. My life will never again be what it once was."

I wanted to erase time for that man, no matter how "terrible" he was.

Surprise Me

"Hey, cutie," a voice said when I picked up the phone. "Ready for your first day of school?"

I knew who it was without asking.

"You make it sound like I'm starting kindergarten."

"Get ready," he said, "Freshman Foundation might feel like kindergarten. Who's your teacher?"

"Ed Gilloggley."

"Ed's the best. He's such a gas. I took a drawing class with him last semester. Are you in the Garage?"

Outside, a car blasting a hip-hop beat sped by.

"You mean the Van Gogh Garage?"

"There's no other."

"Then yes."

"I'm right on your way home." His voice warmed me from the inside out.

"What are *you* starting tomorrow?"

"My job at the computer lab," he said. "I'll get to fiddle around at the main desk when nobody needs my help. You know, you should come by sometime. After class or during lunch or something. I bet it gets lonely there."

"When do you have class?"

"Painting from Life? Second half of the week."

"You're so lucky you get to take painting."

"Sorry, honey," he said. "Freshmen have to wait a year."

"But I've been painting all my life," I sighed. "Doesn't that count for *anything*?"

"You'll play with the big boys soon enough."

"Next year *isn't* soon enough." I hoped I didn't sound too whiney.

He took a breath like he was going to say something, then stopped.

"What were you gonna say?"

"I was just thinking, I can't wait to see you again."

"Me too."

"Let's make it soon."

"Okay," I said, "Want to set a time?"

"No," he whispered. "Surprise me."

Erasing Melodrama

That night I sat in bed, sketching *Ivan the Terrible* from memory.

I thought back to the day I'd first seen him. I'd bought a red

T-shirt and worn it out of the store. It was the first time since fifth grade I'd owned a garment that wasn't black.

When I got home, I stormed into my room and took all my paintings off the walls. I couldn't stand looking at my work anymore, after having seen *Ivan*. My figures looked like cartoon characters in comparison. Ivan got your empathy; my paintings did nothing except beg for attention.

I put the paintings in piles and shoved them under my bed.

Then I went to the bathroom and washed off my makeup. The gray water was sucked to its doom down the drain.

Enough with painting my face; that would just take time and energy away from painting canvases. I needed to learn as much as possible before school started. The other NECAD kids were probably way ahead of me.

At dinner that night, my dad asked, "What's with the red? Are you out of mourning?"

"No," I snapped. "I just never knew I liked red before. And I was never *in* mourning anyway. Can't I do *anything* without you questioning it?"

Right after I said it, I wished I could've taken it back; if I wanted my words to have impact, I'd have to use them more subtly, too. No more emotional outbreaks.

"Cool it, Ellie," my mom said, shaking her head.

My dad just ignored me and resumed cutting his chicken into bite-size pieces. He was used to me overreacting.

"Sorry," I said, as unsarcastically as possible.

As I sat sketching Ivan's eyes the night before my first NECAD class, I realized I had been a little melodramatic in my attempt to erase melodrama.

Foundation Voyage

When I walked into class, Ed Gilloggley was standing on top of a high table, trying to set up floodlights on white geometrical solids so the shadows would be dramatic. But he was short, and it was hard for him to reach the bars on the ceiling, even with the help of a broomstick. Finally he stood on the tallest rectangular block and secured the clamps. He was whistling so hard he had vibrato, like Disney birds.

"There we go! I've got it!" he shouted at the lightbulbs.

I was the first one there. Ed continued his monologue with the lamps. "Here they come! I can hear their footsteps!" Then he looked at me. "I pulled these out of my closet last night," he exclaimed, pointing at the blocks. "They were so dirty I had to paint them white. I was afraid they wouldn't dry in time, but I stuck them in the oven and they did! Look at those shadows!" He sprang off the table and landed lightly on the floor. His wispy comb-over flopped to the wrong side of his head, exposing a circular bald spot.

The Van Gogh Garage was a huge studio off the side of Van Gogh House, an old funeral home turned dorm. The sinks in the Garage were human-body-size. Heavy woodshop machinery lined one of the walls. A thin layer of sawdust covered the floor. It must not have been mopped since last semester.

Not far behind me was a tall guy clunking in two-inch soles, keys jangling on a belt clip. Everything he wore matched, from scarf to pants to argyle socks. He scanned the room with a scrunched nose as if he smelled something rancid.

Next came a mopey guy with hunched shoulders and dragging feet. He carried a bag of Dunkin' Donuts and walked as if he was being towed by a rope attached to his collar. His head was covered with a miserable attempt to grow dirty blond dreads, which stuck out beneath a plaid sagging cap. The crotch in his jeans was about five notches too low and he wore wool socks beneath Birkenstock sandals.

"They're all here! Everybody, have a seat!" Ed shouted as he worked out the setup's finishing touches and gathered his papers.

We each found our way to a paint-encrusted metal stool. They were like the stools we had in grade school, but taller and with a backrest.

The mopey guy left his bulky coat and ratty army backpack on. The backpack pushed him forward in his seat.

"Ten! Nine! Eight! Seven! Six! Five! Four! Three! Two! One! Beeeeeeeeeeeeeeeep! Ready or not, it's time to begin!" Ed seemed to be shouting to make up for what he lacked in size.

The matching boy looked at me. He quickly turned to the mopey guy, then back to me again. Mopey guy stared straight at Ed, never altering his frontal slouch.

"Now, my fine young friends!" Ed shouted, standing on his

toes. "Allow me to give you some background to this Foundation voyage you are about to embark upon!" He pronounced *voyage* the French way.

Mopey guy pulled his cap further over his face, putting his eyes in shadow. The bag of doughnuts rested in his lap.

"It is my job, as your Foundation teacher, to teach you the basic skills of drawing." He drew an imaginary picture with the pencil in his hand. "Two-D design." He waved a piece of paper in the air. "And three-D design!" He lifted a block from the setup on the table.

I wondered if the inside of Ed's body was actually made of gears and switches and little blinking lights. I got the feeling that if he stopped moving he would automatically deactivate, never to start up again.

"You three may not realize it, but you are in a very special situation!" he continued. "You all were deferred for a semester, so during Wintersession I have to catch you up with the rest of your class. You may envy the other students for being allowed to choose any course from the catalog for these six weeks. And you may also think, Six weeks? That's not much time! But you have the advantage of my undivided attention every day we are together. That is very rare! My attention is usually divided between fifteen or twenty students. By the end of Wintersession, you will be more than prepared to join your fellow freshmen for Foundation Two, and if I dare say so, you may learn more than they did in an entire semester!"

Matching boy sneezed three times in a row. He reached into his pants pocket for a red handkerchief, which just happened to be the same color as the stripes on his sweater.

"Bless you! Bless you! Bless you!" Ed shouted.

"Thanks," said matching boy.

"Now for attendance!"

Ed treated taking attendance like it was an audition for a Broadway production. Even though there were only three of us, he prepared for each name by taking a new stance and clearing his throat. He used his entire body. And, like all teachers, he gave us the introductory disclaimer: "I will try my best with pronunciations, but do not hesitate to correct me if I'm wrong. And *please* notify me of any nicknames!"

By my second year in high school all my teachers knew that I went by Ellie. I hadn't had to deal with new reactions to my name in a while.

Ed began, hand over his heart, after a deep breath:

"Ralph LaLande!"

This was matching boy. Apparently, his name was pronounced "Rolph," like the muppet. He sneezed three times after correcting his name. Again, Ed blessed him three times.

Next on the list was Samuel Slant. Mopey guy raised one finger to indicate his presence. "Sam," he said, almost inaudibly. He was munching his way through a chocolate glazed doughnut.

And last but not least was, in the words of Ed Gilloggley, "The one, the only . . . Ladybug Yelinsky!"

Every time I hear my full name spoken by a stranger I want to say, Please forgive my parents; they were tripping when they did this to me.

Mutual Hallucination

My parents named me after a mutual hallucination they had while tripping on acid. They didn't even know each other yet. Later that year they met at a party and discovered they'd had the same hallucination about ladybugs on a bathroom floor at exactly the same time on April 1. My dad says the bugs were crawling but my mom says they were dead. Sometimes when they're telling the story my dad will compromise and say they were sleeping, but my mom will wink and mouth the word *dead*. They named me Ladybug, but they mostly called me L.B., which, through several misunderstandings early in my education, became Ellie.

To Wear the Sunset

On our first break the three of us trudged up the hill to the dining hall, Sam and his backpack dragging behind me and Ralph. Ralph was having a sneezing fit, always in sets of three. His keys jingled with each step.

"I'm allergic to sawdust," he said, fanning his fingers in front of his nose. "And that spastic teacher jumping around doesn't help one bit." He went on to complain about how the charcoal Ed was making us buy would mess up his shirt. And what if he had an itch while he was drawing? Would I promise to tell him if he had charcoal-face?

After filling our trays, we waited in line to pay.

"Oh, Ellie," Ralph sighed, playing with the keys in his pocket. "I hadn't pegged you as a carnivore."

I looked at my grilled chicken sandwich.

"Sam I could've guessed. But not you."

Sam readjusted his cap and glared at Ralph.

"You just met us," I said. "How could you know anything about us?"

"Just a hunch," he said. "And my hunches are usually right."

We slid our trays closer to the cashier.

"Have you ever considered veganism?" Ralph asked.

"No," I said. "I've never heard of it."

"Absolutely no animal products," he said proudly. "No eggs, no cheese, and obviously no meat."

The cash register dinged as it rang up Ralph's salad.

"Really, Ellie," he said, "it's the most humane and healthy way to eat."

We found a table by the windows. I sat across from both guys.

Sam finally removed his backpack. I was relieved. I'd started to think he was hiding a large back tumor in there.

"Do you two know what you want to major in?" Ralph asked.

"Film," Sam said, engrossed in his bacon cheeseburger. His voice was so deep it sounded like someone had turned the speed knob way down on his voice box.

"Painting," I said.

"Painting," Ralph repeated. "So this Foundation stuff will actually be useful for you!"

"What do you mean?" I asked. "Isn't it useful for everyone?"

"Oh, no no no," Ralph said, shaking his index finger. "I'm going into apparel. Drawing and three-D design have nothing, absolutely nothing, to do with apparel. All the sketches clothing designers make are completely stylized. The only thing I can use is two-D design. That is, *if* this Gilloggley guy can stay still long enough to teach. Foundation class is just something I have to get through."

"Right on," Sam said. "Can't wait for next year. That's when school really begins." He sipped his Coke. Some of the soda spilled on his shirt. He glanced up to see if I noticed.

I turned to Ralph. "Why did you choose fashion design?"

He finished swallowing a bite of well-chewed mixed salad greens before answering. "Well, Ellie, I believe that the purest form of art is *apparel* design — in the fashion industry, we prefer the term *apparel*. When you wear art, you *become* the art. With all other mediums, you experience the art indirectly."

"What kind of clothes do you design?" I asked.

"Recently, I've been developing a you-are-the-environment approach to apparel," Ralph said, gesturing toward the window.

Sam looked up to see my reaction.

I remained poker-faced. "You are the environment?"

"Ellie, did you ever see a sunset so beautiful you wanted to wear it?"

Sam rolled his eyes so only I could see.

"I like sunsets," I said.

"By the time we graduate from NECAD, you will be able to wear the sunset," he assured me.

Sam stopped chewing his cheeseburger and widened his heavy eyes so much that the whites seemed to glow beneath the shadow from his cap.

Generational Revisions

"But Ed, Ellie's going to be a painting major," Ralph said. "Don't you think at least *she* should get to paint?"

"Good point, Ralph. But here in Foundation class, we all start at the same place. We begin with the basics! You'd probably be surprised, even with the talent you all have, how much you don't know!"

"Like what?" Ralph asked.

Eye roll from Sam.

"For starters," Ed said, ripping off the cover to a huge pad of newsprint, "I bet none of you know how to draw those blocks correctly!" He pointed at the block setup on the table.

"I bet we do," said Ralph. "We came here to learn more complicated stuff."

"All in good time, Ralph!" Ed shouted while securing the newsprint pad to an easel. "For now, let's stick to the blocks. Now, everybody! Please direct your attention over here as I create a three-dimensional form using only this piece of charcoal and this piece of paper."

Ed drew a few lines in the shape of a cube. Then he held a knitting needle at arm's length from his face and squinted at the blocks. He redrew his lines, then erased the old ones.

"Even an old pro like me makes mistakes! This is great for you all to see! Remember, the eraser can be your most powerful tool. I don't care if you have seventy-four wrong lines showing through, as long as you finally get the right one!"

As Ed corrected his lines, I wondered if Ralph was right. I didn't come here to learn how to draw blocks; I came to learn how to paint. What was the use of being in this class if Ed wasn't even going to teach us the fundamentals of painting?

Ever since I was old enough to use crayons and finger paint, I had wanted to go to NECAD. My mother had etched in my brain that it was the best art school in the country. If she could do her life over again, she would've gone here.

It was the only school I applied to, because I figured I wouldn't be happy anywhere else. But maybe at other schools, you didn't have to sit through block demonstrations.

This class was a far cry from the anatomical drawing class my mom took at the Art Student's League when I was young. I used to spend a lot of time pawing through the pages in her portfolio case, tracing the drawn bones and muscles with my finger. She told me the teacher had said she really had a future in art.

"So in effect, you are paying these people to take off their clothes," my dad would say when she came home from class.

"Yes, I'm sure they wouldn't do it for free," Mom would answer.

"But would they make as much if they kept their clothes on?" he'd ask. "I bet you all could be saving some money if you brought this to the attention of the administration."

They were tight for cash, since Dad was in law school. He encouraged my mom to use her creative talents to make money. She taught herself how to stencil and faux finish so she could fix up fancy apartments. Her customers were guaranteed to be wealthy. Eventually she was able to make any paintable surface look like any type of wood or stone.

It wasn't only for him that she withdrew from fine art, she told me; it was fun going into strangers' homes and completely changing the mood of the place. But she also said I shouldn't follow in her footsteps. I had more talent and it would be sinful to waste it.

Well, I hadn't planned on wasting it. That was the jumpy guy in the front of the room's fault.

Book of Bones

By the end of class I was so fed up with Ed's basics that I ran up the hill and through the quad arches to the NECAD library. They had a whole section on anatomy. Some of the books were for artists and some were medical. I recognized most of them from the library in New York. I picked out my favorite: *Human Anatomy for Artists* by Eliot Goldfinger.

I settled down with it on a fuzzy blue couch. There weren't many people in the library, but every footstep and closing book echoed through the cavernous room. The overhead lights didn't do much to brighten the place, but there were antique lamps at every table and beside every couch. The high ceiling was patterned with skylights.

Goldfinger's book made anatomy look more simple than Leonardo's drawings. Plus, it was written in English and from left to right. But it wasn't the English most of us learn to speak; there were so many technical terms, it was almost like reading a foreign language. *Anterior* meant front view, *posterior,* back view, and *lateral,* side view. Then there were different types of movement: *flexion* and *extension; inversion* and *eversion; abduction* and *adduction.* I couldn't keep them all straight.

The names of the bones sounded like titles for prehistoric royalty: The Great Trochanter, Corocoid the Almighty, Princess Phalanges.

I took off my shoes, lay back, and placed my feet on the arm of the couch. Darkness fell over the skylights.

I held the book up to the lamp. I couldn't get enough of the pictures. Goldfinger made line drawings showing the basic geometry of the bones. Then, beside those diagrams, were drawings of the muscles that lay on top of the bones. Next there were photographs of real people, showing what the muscles looked like with skin on top.

This is what Ed should be teaching us, I thought.

But there wasn't anything stopping me from learning on my own, so I checked the book out and started running home.

Beyond Second

Before I got home, I stopped and turned back toward the path to Nate's house. Wind was blowing through the creaky bare branches. I walked halfway up the path, not even sure why I was there. I didn't have time to hang out or anything; I had to get up early for class.

His lights were out. I thought I saw his thick hair moving above where his futon would be, but after a few seconds I couldn't see him anymore. Must be a reflection in the window, I thought.

I remembered Nate's lips against my ear. And how he kissed

my body in the night. I wondered what would happen next time I saw him. I had finally gone beyond first base. Beyond second, too. I imagined what it might be like to go all the way with him. Maybe someday we would.

I saw the movement through his window again. But this time it looked like two heads. And one was a girl's. My heart sped up. I walked a few feet closer to the house and squinted at the window for a few minutes. Nothing there.

A gust of wind blew at my face and reminded me how cold it was. I turned back down the path and ran home. The sky was clear and the stars looked like snowflakes stuck in place. I wasn't ready to go inside, to let the cold layer on my throat defrost. I ran a circle around my house, feet stamping the frosty grass.

I tagged stray rocks with my toes as I went, wind slapping my hair across my cheeks.

When I completed the circle, I ran up the steps to my apartment and through the door. Then I collapsed on my bed, heart pounding.

I closed my eyes and tried to imagine the feel of Nate's hair in my hands.

Time to Proceed

"Remember, blocks have thickness!" Ed shouted. "Be sure to include every side that you see." He circled around us.

Ed had arranged our easels at equidistant points around the block setup.

"And no modeling!" he shouted. "Only lines! You'll have plenty of time for modeling later. Modeling is the frosting on the cake!"

Modeling was the word Ed used for rendering the lights and darks. He called it modeling because it created a sculpturesque three-dimensional illusion.

Ed wanted our lines to be perfectly straight. We weren't allowed to use rulers. I wondered if Leonardo had ever drawn from a setup like this. It seemed too simple to be a real art-school assignment.

But it was harder than I'd expected. If you didn't get the base lines at exactly the right angles, the blocks looked like they were floating rather than sitting. If the edges didn't appear to be parallel, you would have a lopsided cube, which really isn't a cube at all. If you didn't give each block enough space, they would look like they were occupying the same space on the table, which is physically impossible.

The class was quiet, other than Ed's constant shuffling around.

As I drew I thought about Nate. About Nate in my bed.

I wondered if I would actually have time to spend with him. Ed had made it clear that he was going to work us hard; lectures and instruction all day and assignments for evenings and weekends. There *must* be time for dating, I thought.

"Yes yes yes, you're almost there, Ellie!" Ed shouted in my ear.

I jumped to the side, breath caught in my throat.

"You see? All it takes is some concentration! Just lower the curve on the bottom of that cone a smidge and watch out for the tall cylinder! It looks like the Leaning Tower of Pisa! Get that worked out and you'll be ready for the next step!"

He moved on to Ralph, whose sky-blue shoes matched the cloud scene on his shirt.

"Achoo-achoo-achoo!"

"Bless you! Bless you! Bless you!"

"Ed, I'm allergic to sawdust," Ralph said accusingly, rubbing the bottom of his nose with one finger.

Ed looked down and kicked at the dust.

Ralph sneezed.

Ed blessed.

"My goodness, you *are* allergic, aren't you!" Ed gasped. "Well, we'll certainly have to do something about that, won't we? At the break, Sam, Ellie, what do you say we mop up this mess for our friend Ralph?"

Sam and I exchanged glances. "Okay," I said. Sam nodded once.

"Terrific!" Ed shouted, then turned back to Ralph. "It's pretty good, Ralph, it's pretty good," he said, pointing at Ralph's drawing. "But that sphere in front looks about eight times bigger than the sphere in the back, and really, they're the same size! And next time you could shrink the whole image by five percent!"

"Five percent?" Ralph asked, shooting me a *Was I the only one who heard that?* look.

"Yes, Ralph," Ed said. "It would give your page more space and it would give your teacher some peace of mind. I feel claustrophobic when I see an image that doesn't have room to breathe!"

"And how are we doing, Sam?" he asked on his way to Sam's easel.

"Okay," Sam mumbled, pulling nervously on the brim of his cap.

"Straighten out those lines, Sam, and you'll be in business. Right now you've got blocks made out of noodles!"

At noon Ed yelled, "Everyone, put down your charcoal and pick up a broom! Everyone except Ralph, that is!" He handed a broom to me and one to Sam, and kept the third for himself. "Ralph, you are free to go if you wish."

But Ralph didn't wish to go. Instead, he stuck around and pointed to spots we'd missed, sneezing all the while. When we had swept every last bit out the garage door, Ed presented us with mops. We filled the buckets in the human-size sinks.

By the time we were soaking the floor, Ralph decided it was safe to leave.

As he left the room, I mopped my way past Sam. He said almost imperceptibly, "That guy needs to take a chill pill."

Ed gave us an extra half hour for lunch because we did such a "sparkling good job." Ralph was finishing the last bites of his spinach salad when we got there. Unlike us, he had to be back on time so he left just as we were sitting down. He didn't even thank us.

Since we had both taken seats facing Ralph, Sam and I were left eating side by side. I was cornered in against the wall, so I thought it was his job to move to the chair across from me. But he stayed where he was, the two of us facing outward as if the dining hall was a play we were watching.

"So Ralph had us working for him today," I said, unable to think of anything less obvious.

"Yeah," Sam said. "Bummer."

From then on chewing was the only noise we made.

I kept sneaking glances at Sam as he munched. He had the most well-defined masseter muscle I'd ever seen.

We had finished eating before the half hour was up.

"Do you want to head back?" I asked.

"Okay," Sam said.

He snatched an apple from the fruit bin on our way out, when no one was looking. You weren't supposed to take any food out of the dining hall.

As we walked down the hill, Sam said, "You're quiet. Like me."

"I'm not really quiet," I said. "I just can't think of anything to say."

He handed me his apple. "You want this?" he asked. "I'm not hungry."

"Why not." I chomped on it the entire way back. It kept me from having to invent conversation with him.

For the next couple of hours, we worked out our drawings' imperfections. Ed circled around, giving us advice.

After six or seven rounds, Ed entered the center of the room and stood by the blocks.

"Everybody!" he announced, extending both arms as if offering us a gift. "It is time to proceed! Proceed to the modeling!!"

You would think, from the expression on his face, that he'd just told us we had won the lottery.

A Realistic Tree

I should've known better than to wear brown pants and a green shirt to the studio. It was our third day of Foundation, and we were working in the evening on our first out-of-class assignment.

Ralph's face lit up like an ambulance on the run.

"Ellie, you're a tree!" he exclaimed, as if I had dressed just to please his freaky fashion sense.

Sam was on his way out.

"Leaving already?" I asked.

"Gotta get dinner," he said, pulling on his cap. "Haven't left since class."

Ed wanted us to draw compositions from the blocks, which he had rearranged in a new setup. The assignment was to imagine cutting geometric chunks out of the shapes in our drawings, making sure they looked perspectively correct. When we had all the lines right we could begin to model the drawing. We had to keep our invented lighting inside the holes consistent with the lighting on the forms' exteriors.

"Remember, the shadow is always darkest when it is closest to the light!" Ed had reminded us that day in class.

It was a pretty mechanical process, and I soon forgot that Ralph was standing at the easel beside me.

But he stopped drawing after about two hours and turned in my direction, hands on his hips and nodding. My drawing had just begun to come into focus, and I was almost ready to plan where I'd be cutting into my blocks. Ralph hovered around me, eying me from head to toe and squinting as if he was doing calculus in his head.

"There could be branches coming out of the shoulders. We'd be sure to place them where they wouldn't obstruct your vision. And we could hint at roots growing out of your shoes! I wonder if you could weave actual wood into the fabric — little pieces like in Chinese curtains!"

My lack of response encouraged him to continue. As if maybe I didn't get it yet.

"Wouldn't that be great? You could be a tree! I mean, you're close now, but you could be a *realistic* tree!"

"Yeah, a tree would be perfect," I said flatly, still staring at my easel.

He must have been insulted because he stopped talking. He was harder to tolerate without Sam there. Whenever Ralph got annoying I could always count on an eye roll from Sam.

Ralph gave up, and we both got sucked in by the display of cubes, spheres, and cones and our mission to convincingly remove pieces from them. For a long time my thoughts revolved around words like *space, line,* and *perspective.* Every once in a while Nate entered my mind and at those moments I wanted to be lying in bed with him, to feel his breath on my neck. But I forced myself to concentrate on the assignment.

Then Ralph piped up again.

"Check it out, Ellie!" he cried. "This piece I just cut out looks *exactly* like Mickey Mouse, and I didn't even do it on purpose!"

"Oh, wonderful," I sighed.

I wanted to feel Nate's hair in my hands. And his lips on my ear. So much that my lines weren't coming out straight anymore. There were ghosts of about sixteen erased marks in one spot where my accuracy had failed. Standing there, looking at my drawing but not really seeing it, I knew it was time to escape the world of Ralph LaLande.

It seemed silly to go home and call before heading over, when I'd be passing his house on my way. And anyway, he'd asked for a surprise.

I ran straight to his apartment.

What Makes It Crazy

Nate was on the phone when I arrived. I waded through the fire hydrants and took a seat on his futon. He paced from the doorway to the stove to the night table and back to the doorway again. Each time he retraced his path he placed his feet in almost exactly the same spots as the time before, always avoiding the sculptures.

The radiator was banging.

"This isn't a good time," he said to the person on the other line.

Pause.

"No, no. Yes I want to, but not now."

Pause. The dim light flickered.

"No, look, I have a guest." He winked at me.

I leaned back and glued my eyes to the ceiling, to make it seem like I wasn't listening. The molding was tinged brown and the paint was peeling.

"Oh, come on."

Pause.

"Yeah, okay. Tomorrow. Bye. You too."

His hang-up bordered on a slam.

"Is something wrong?" I asked.

"No," he said. "It's just this old high school friend. We fight a lot."

The scar moved in unison with his mouth as he spoke.

The little men were hammering hard inside his radiator.

I wanted to shut it off.

Nate held out his hand, and I grabbed on with both of mine as he hoisted me up. His tight rocking squeeze molded me against his body. He put his lips on the hair that covered my ear and said, "I missed you. I know I just met you, but I missed you."

His fingers crept inside the back of my shirt, and I did the same to him. He kissed me long and slow, and before his lips left mine he reached behind my head and flipped the light switch off. In the dark, he began a new kiss and put his hands on my waist and gradually lifted my shirt. His hands were like parentheses around my body, pushing my shirt up and continuing over my raised arms until they got to my fingertips. He tried to unhook my bra. After letting him fumble a little while, I did it for him.

I took his shirt off the same way he had removed mine.

We were still standing near the futon. He tackled me to the mattress.

His touches were like hot air blowing over my skin. But his kisses were rushed, like he was racing to some abstract finish line.

I reached around him and ran my fingers up and down his spine, slowing down for each bump along the way. Then I moved out to the sides. Over ribs, scapulas. I had always thought of backs as being flat, but there in the dark I couldn't find a single flat spot on it. My favorite part on him was the curve between his scapulas. They stuck out like handles, like they were meant for grabbing on to.

He planted kisses all over my face and landed on my nose. He bit it softly.

"Be crazy," he said, "make love to me."

"I don't love you and you don't love me," I answered. His face was barely visible, but I could see his eyebrows arching in upside-down smiles.

"That," he said, "is what makes it crazy."

"I don't know." I kissed his eyelids so he couldn't see I was nervous.

"Come on, Ellie. It'll be fun. I have condoms, if that's what you're worried about."

That was the only thing I was worried about, right? Protection and sobriety, that was it. Sobriety, just to make sure I really wanted to do what I was doing. Maybe Nate didn't love me, but he seemed to *like* me a whole lot. I always told myself I had to do it with the right guy. Someone who would take it seriously, who wouldn't forget about me afterward. He seems like he could be the right guy, I thought.

I had to think fast because he was unzipping my jeans.

Almost all the girls I knew in high school had already lost their virginity. I guess it shouldn't have felt like such a big deal. This was the moment I'd wondered about and looked forward to for so long, but I'd imagined it unfolding differently. Slower.

Plus, how could I say no at this point? He'd think I didn't like him. Or maybe he wouldn't like me anymore.

I wriggled my legs to help him get my pants down and over my feet. He took care of removing the rest of my clothes and his.

He pulled the blankets over us and held me, both of us completely naked.

Once you're naked, there's no turning back, I thought.

"You okay?" he asked.

"Yeah."

"You sure?"

"Mmhmm."

He began and I followed his lead. At first he had trouble getting in. Then he ran his tongue over my neck and chest like he was drawing a maze, and it got easier. The beginning part felt all right. But the farther we went, the more it seemed like we were two incompatible machines that someone had experimentally hooked together and then pushed go. And his machine was definitely winning.

The pain was a weird kind of good pain. I wasn't sure if I wanted him to keep going or not, but at this point I felt like it was too late to tell him to stop.

It was over before I knew it. He rolled off me and onto his back and pulled me close so my head could rest on his chest. His heart was pounding against my face and he was sweating.

Then he sat up and ripped the blankets off the bed.

"What are you doing!" I said louder than I meant to.

"Stand up." He held his comforter out like a cape.

"Why?" I asked, curled up in a shivering ball.

"Just do it," he said, "and you'll be warm."

When I rose, he wrapped the blanket around me. Then he peeled a corner back and joined me in the cocoon. He took my hand and started for the door.

"Outside?" I asked, holding back.

But my feet kept moving because Nate and the blanket were pulling me.

"It's too hot in here," he said. "We need fresh air."

It wasn't as cold outside as I'd expected. But the ground was frosty and I walked on my toes. The sky was so light, the street lamps were irrelevant.

We sat on his front steps watching our smoke breath disappear into the night.

My feet snuck inside the blanket, leaving only my head exposed.

Then out of nowhere it began to snow. Hard.

"Is that *snow*?" Nate asked.

"Of course it's snow," I said. "What did you think it was?"

"I've never seen snow." He tilted his head back to let the quarter-size flakes fall in his mouth.

"SNOOOOOOWWW!" he yelled, leaping off the steps and dashing down the path, leaving me feeling very clothed in my blanket. It was coming down so heavily his hair was completely white, like a mammoth attack of dandruff. He ran back toward me, limbs flailing in all directions.

His arms and legs weren't the only parts of him that were flopping around.

"Let me in! Let me in!" he called in a crackly pubescent voice.

All of his muscles were well defined, like the diagrams in *Human Anatomy for Artists*.

I stood and opened up a side for him. He shook out his snow-covered hair, spraying me in the face. I was about to play-slap him, but he had wrapped himself around me, and I was paralyzed by his freezing wetness.

He pulled me, arm around my waist, to the path, which was quickly fading to white. My feet stung so much I could hardly feel them, had no control over which direction they were going. Nate ran us into the wooded area, weaving between trees. Well, we were half running, half hopping because of all the rocks and fallen branches. He was whooping and I was laughing. Twigs snapped beneath my feet. He brought us back around to the house, but instead of going up the steps, he pushed me against the brick building. He pinned me with his pelvis and leaned his head back to catch a mouthful of snow.

Then he snow-kissed me. His mouth was gentle and cold, and he rolled his tongue around mine while the snow melted in my mouth.

It was so silent, we seemed to be surrounded by the absence of sound, as if the freshly falling flakes absorbed everything audible.

The snow was dying down and I really thought I might not have feet anymore. Nate marched us back inside to warmth and dry blankets.

Convincingly Cut

It was so dark when the alarm started screeching, I couldn't believe it was morning. Rain had pounded the snow out of sight. I didn't want to move, become separate from the bed. But if I didn't get up soon, I'd be late for class. No, I was already late. There wasn't time to go home and change. I'd have to make my second appearance as a tree. I'd tell Ralph my clothes didn't dry in the dryer last night.

I told Nate we had to get up, but he rolled onto his stomach and pulled the covers over his head like a snail being poked. He could stay there, but a teacher notices when one of three is missing.

There was so much rain flowing on the pavement, the sewers couldn't suck it up fast enough. People rushed through the water-fall streets, their drawing boards in huge plastic bags. Luckily, my class was allowed to leave our stuff on racks in the room.

At first my coat saved only my upper half, and served as a slide for the rain to land on my thighs. Passing vehicles seemed to take pleasure in splashing cold slushy puddles against my side. The water had soaked through my jacket by the time I got to the Garage.

Ralph and Sam had already pinned their drawings on the wall.

"Welcome, Ellie!" Ed shouted. "You are just in time for our first crit! I was telling Sam, here, that I was hoping you weren't sick."

He wasn't even being sarcastic.

I hung my drawing with the others.

"Look at the shapes, the negative space! Your progress is astounding!" Ed raced back and forth in front of our pieces.

He went on, analyzing each one individually. But my heavy head was bobbing as if my neck was made of rubber and couldn't support the weight of my brain. What I caught of Ed's crit sounded something like, "Rendered blah blah can you see how the planes and the angle with the blah blah blah captured perspective oh look at blah blah to the vanishing point! And blah blah BLAH, what do you think, Ellie?"

That was my name.

He still looked just as excited as ever.

I recrossed my legs in the other direction and looked from drawing to drawing, first taking in the picture as a whole, then focusing on the details. I scrunched my face up, hoping to appear as if I was considering everything he'd been discussing, rather than figuring out what he was asking. "Hey, guys, guess where my virginity is! I left it back at Nate Finerman's house!" was all that came to my head.

"I think . . . he cut the shapes out very convincingly," I said.

"Yes. Yes! Didn't he? You wouldn't know they were whole to begin with! Good job, Ralph!"

And so the morning went. Luckily he didn't ask me any more questions. At least not in front of Ralph and Sam.

On a break, Ed asked me if I was feeling okay. "There's something a little un-Ellie about you today," he said.

"I'm fine," I told him. "I just didn't sleep much last night."

"That'll do it," Ed said, a little quieter than usual. "When I have trouble sleeping, I drink a mug of hot milk. I can't work without enough sleep. Try milk next time." Then he turned to the rest of the class. "Everybody!" he announced. "Let's take lunch!"

I wondered if Nate had gone to class. Maybe I should go to the painting building and get him to have lunch with me, I thought. No, the next time I see him we should have some privacy. Plus, we'd need time to talk.

Instead of finding Nate, I went to the dining hall with Ralph and Sam.

When we returned, Ed had set up a still life with fruit and bottles that he had painted in varied tones of gray for our practice. Even the apple was gray. At least we were on our way to drawing real things. It seemed ridiculous to me that I couldn't be painting like Nate, or at least drawing people.

"Does anyone notice anything special about these grays?" Ed shouted.

No answer.

Ed pulled out a piece of cardboard with gray squares on it, fading from white to black. "There are nine values on here! And the values decrease in whole steps! See?! The square in the middle is exactly the average of black and white. And each of the squares is the average of the two squares that surround it!"

I didn't want to be in the Garage, and couldn't imagine being there until six. I needed to know what Nate was feeling now, if he regretted it, if he'd ever want to talk to me again. Like in the movies, when the guy just uses the girl for sex and never calls. Maybe I should've waited.

The next thing I heard Ed say was, "Check this out, Ellie! Which one do you think it is?!"

"Um, it's the one . . . in the . . ."

Ralph covered his mouth to hold back a laugh. Sam peeked at me from under his cap.

"That's correct, Ellie! The tall bottle on the right is the middle value!"

"That's the one I meant," I said.

"Of course it was!"

The tail end of a laugh escaped through Ralph's cupped hand.

I wondered if I should go to Nate's right after class, or if I should go later, or if I should even go at all. I wanted to see him, but I didn't want to seem clingy. And what if I showed up and it turned out that he *had* changed his mind about me?

But when six o'clock rolled around, I found myself running straight through the freezing mist to his house.

Last-Minute Self-Portrait

I rang the buzzer.

He opened the door just enough to stick his head between it and the frame.

"I'm on my way out," he said.

His first assignment, a self-portrait, was due tomorrow, so he had to go to the painting building to work on it. He said he didn't get work done last night for obvious reasons.

"You sure you're not offended?" he asked, rubbing my cheek with his thumb.

It hadn't occurred to me to be offended until he brought it up. That's why we were in school. To get work done.

I wondered if he really had work to do, or if he didn't want to see me.

I headed home. The brown slush of the day had frozen fast with the setting sun. A girl ahead of me on the sidewalk slipped and fell on her butt. Her gluteus maximus. I jumped over an ice puddle and walked on the tire-marked road, where my boots could grip the ground.

At home I cooked myself some mac and cheese, and scribbled

copies of pictures from *Human Anatomy for Artists* in my sketch-book.

That night I climbed into my bed as a nonvirgin for the first time. Until yesterday there was always this open-ended wondering about when and where and *if* it would happen. Now there was one less word that could be used to describe me.

All You Need to Know

I lay in bed for hours that night, wishing I could turn back the universal clock and get some sleep. Maybe I should've cooked up some milk. As if that would really work.

I was thinking about Nate. And his dad. Nate never got a father-son sex talk — an experience I thought all boys were supposed to have. Unfortunately, my dad tried to have a father-daughter sex talk with me. Back when I had no concept of what sex really was.

"What do they teach you in sexual education?" he asked me after dinner one night. He made it sound so official. At school we all said "sex ed."

"I don't know," I said. I was rummaging through my mom's high school yearbook. I was looking for a guy with dark wild hair. I'd seen him in some pictures that I found in a shoebox under my mom's side of the bed and I wanted to know his name. Mom was at her gold leafing class.

"I can't believe they start you in on this in sixth grade." He peered over his glasses.

I shrugged.

That was our first-year meeting with Ms. Tittlebaum. After lunch for a week, the girls and boys were separated into different rooms, which was supposed to make us feel more "comfortable." The first day, Ms. Tittlebaum had drawn a gigantic penis on the chalkboard and asked us if we knew any nicknames for it. It was pretty hard to feel comfortable, even with only girls in the class. Nobody raised her hand.

"I'll tell you all you need to know about sexual intercourse," my dad said.

"Please don't." I found a picture of a guy with wild hair, but not the right face.

"Hold on to your virginity. Hold on with all your might. Those high school boys have only one thing on their mind. Trust me, I was one once."

I scrunched my face at him. "That's gross. Don't tell me things like that."

There were a few guys on the next page with *his* hairstyle. It must've been in back then.

"Well, what do *they* tell you about?" he asked.

"Puberty. You know, growing hair and stuff."

One guy left a note, "Love You Always," by his picture, but he was all skinny and geeky looking. Couldn't be him.

"How about protection? Are they teaching you about that?"

Sure they were. But I wasn't going to tell my dad that Ms.

Tittlebaum had brought in condoms and that we'd all passed them around the room like we were playing hot potato.

"Okay, you don't have to answer," he said, smiling. "I can see that yearbook's way more interesting than your old man. Find any of Mom's friends?"

"Some, I guess."

He *had* to be in here. Maybe I'd skipped a page somewhere.

"Mom's got all sorts of ex-boyfriends in there," he said. "But I won her in the end!"

I turned back to the first page to start again.

He sat, watching me, for maybe ten minutes. He got fidgety — bouncing his knee and tapping the table. I pretended he wasn't there.

"What are you doing, anyway?" he finally asked.

"Just looking for someone, okay?" I said. "Not that it's any of your business."

He took off his glasses and sneered at me. "I was only asking a question," he said firmly.

"And I was only answering."

He sat back and fumed.

"Who are you looking for?" he asked after a long silence. "Your real dad?" Suddenly his eyes looked stunned, as if he couldn't believe those words had escaped his mouth. He took a deep breath and let out a forced chuckle. "Or do you have a crush on someone in there?"

I didn't join his laughter.

He put his hand on top of mine, sandwiching it against the yearbook. "I'm just teasing," he said. "You know that, right?"

His hand was shaking.

The Gilloggley Workout

Friday morning, Ed had set up a table full of dilapidated violins. He put on a tape of Tchaikovsky's Violin Concerto in D as inspiration. I recognized the melody, but had never known what it was called. I wrote it down in my sketchbook so I'd remember to buy it. I had always thought of classical as background music. Easy to tune out. But the piece was so intense it was hard to concentrate on drawing.

Ed was doing a composition analysis, jumping from person to person. He wanted us to make the negative shapes, the spaces around the violins, dynamic.

"Negative and positive shapes must play off one another!" he shouted. "And in this case, I mean it literally!" He bowed his air violin in sweeping strokes as he laughed. He circled around, giving a few tips here and there, but soon he stepped back and let us work. For a while, all we heard from Ed were Disney whistles mimicking the violin concerto.

Ralph and I stood at easels, but Sam sat hunched over a desk. Headphones on, select dreads peeking out from under his hat.

At the end of the concerto's first movement Ed stopped behind Sam and said, "Hey, Sam, what's playing?"

Sam kept sketching, like there was another Sam in the room and Ed was definitely talking to that one.

Ed scuttled in front of him.

"Sam! Sam!" He waved his arms around, adding occasional jumps to his flailing.

At this point, Ralph and I didn't even attempt to stifle our laughter. And when Ralph started laughing, he had a hard time stopping. He also had a hard time not sounding like a girl experiencing mild hysteria.

With a look that seemed to say, "Get this, guys!" Ed burst into fully fledged jumping jacks, shouting Sam's name in time, combover flopping with each jump.

"SAM! SAM! SAM! SAM!"

Finally, Ed knelt down and stuck his face in front of Sam's to get his attention.

"What's playing, Sam?" he asked, just as energized as the first time.

"What?" Sam said, not removing his headphones. He looked Ed in the eye without moving his head.

"What are you listening to?" Ed pointed to his own ears, just in case Sam didn't understand.

"Phish," Sam said. His mouth barely moved when he spoke.

"Fish? Fish! Sam, what a good idea! I will have to get fish for you guys to draw next week! Just picture their color, their texture, their movement! Sam, you are wonderful!"

Sam's unmoving eyes seemed to refuel Ed's energy, as if they were mirrors reflecting it right back into him.

"And Sam!" Ed shouted as he jumping-jacked back to the setup.

"Yeah," Sam answered dryly.

"Thanks for the workout!"

High School Friend

I walked to the computer lab after class, thinking maybe I'd run into Nate. But he was nowhere in sight, so I decided to make use of my new e-mail account while I was in the building. Nate must check his messages often, since he works here, I thought. I wanted to tell him how much I liked lying beside him and feeling him in the dark. But I didn't want to sound like a cheezeball.

For a few minutes I twisted in semicircles on a swivel chair, watching the cursor blink back at me, before I came up with anything.

Finally I wrote:

> Nate,
> You have the best back in the world, and I feel privileged that you let me touch it. I know that sounds silly, but it's true and there's no other way to express it.
> Looking forward to our next encounter,
> Ellie

It was warmer than usual outside. The campus was still slushy from all that rain and melted snow.

Going up the hill, I recognized Nate's electric hairstyle.

He was walking with some girl. Half of her head was shaved to a dark stubble. The other half of her hair was bleached blond and came to her chin. She kept flipping it out of her eyes.

"Ellie!" he said overenthusiastically. "This is Clarissa. She's visiting for the weekend from NYU. She's my, you know —" He smiled sheepishly and looked back and forth from her to me. "My um —"

"Girlfriend," she said curtly, shoving her hand in my direction for a shake.

Her hand felt like a limp flounder.

She looked my charcoal-covered body up and down, as if I were a cute little dress she was thinking of buying. A miniature backpack clung to her shoulders over her leather jacket. Her black boots laced all the way up to her knees. There they were met by the hem of a leopard-print skirt.

"You should come over sometime," Nate said, glancing back and forth from me to Clarissa. "I bet you two would hit it off."

"I have to go home now," I said. I tried to form the words clearly, but they came out all wavery. I wanted Nate to wink or give some sign that Clarissa was delusional — that maybe *she* thought she was his girlfriend, but he was merely humoring her. All I got was his usual grin and her footsteps clacking into the distance.

Where the F@#! We're Looking

When I was sure they were around the corner and out of sight, I ran to my house. My head throbbed. I had heard of people who drank to forget. No, the best thing to do would be to keep running. Running and running until the name *Nate* meant nothing to me. But I'm not *that* much of an athlete. I don't think my feet could've taken me far enough.

I did have wheels though.

I bolted down the stairs to the basement, where my bike was locked. I didn't even wait to get to the street before I got on. I wanted to pump my thoughts out as I stood on the pedals, pushing through the slushy mud. By the time I got off the grass I was in a rhythm, booking down the sidewalk.

I wished more than anything that I could enter cyberspace and delete that stupid e-mail.

Tears stuck to the walls of my throat. It hurt to keep them from spouting out of my eyes, but I forced them back anyway.

I should've known that Nate didn't *really* like me, that he only wanted me for my body.

I did know. And now I wouldn't let him make me cry. He wasn't worth it.

I saw some movement coming from the courtyard ahead and to my left, and it occurred to me a little too late that I should grab my brakes. I came to a screeching halt. My front wheel just barely bumped the leg of a woman in a fur coat. She gasped and looked at me as if I had murdered before her eyes the minks she now clutched around her wide bosom.

"I'm sorry, I'm really sorry," I said.

But her blood-red lips were stuck in a giant O.

From the window of a purple pickup truck, a man called to the mink lady, "Hey, are you okay?"

This broke her from her trance and as she crossed the street she yelled back to him, "I don't know where the *fuck* they're looking, but it ain't ahead!"

We, the bikers of America, are looking ahead, lady. We're just trying to hit you.

Quad Coasting

I may have said I was sorry, but hitting Her Minkness didn't bother me in the least. What upset me more than crashing into mink lady was that I'd been so distracted I didn't see her in time. Just because

I was doing exactly what I had told myself I *wouldn't* do: let Nate get to me.

I continued riding down Artist's Row and turned left on College Street, heading toward the quad on top of the hill. The pedals fought back against my calves as I pumped. By the time I reached the grass, I had slowed down so much I thought I might start rolling backwards.

Hardly anyone was out on the swampy quad as I rode through the brick archway. The administrative buildings were abandoned. The puddled ground looked like it could swallow you up if you walked in it. I stuck to the paths because they were at least slightly shoveled and I could avoid getting splashed by the slushy muck below.

My girlfriend.

I couldn't get the phrase or her face out of my head. I was sure he wouldn't use the same title to describe me. Or even allow me to use the word to describe myself.

I glided down the paths, standing on the pedals, making sharp turns on the corners, using the brakes as little as possible. And then it began to rain. At first the clouds sprinkled me a warning as if to apologize for the inevitable. But before I had time to cross the quad, it was pouring. It might have been mild for winter, but that water could not have been colder without being frozen. So I made my way back home, letting the rain drench my clothes, slather my hair, rush down my face, camouflage the tears I could no longer prevent. Splattering through wide puddles on the quad didn't matter anymore.

Coasting down College Street, I wondered what kind of explanation Nate could have. I didn't think we were "going steady," but I couldn't believe he had a girlfriend. I guess that made me his mistress. Well, not anymore, I thought.

Good luck, Nate Finerman, in getting *me* to sleep over ever again.

Shared Traits

I must have something in common with her, I thought, sitting up in bed that night. If I didn't, he wouldn't like us both.

My sketchbook sat in my lap.

I drew a portrait of Clarissa. Of what I could remember, at least. Then a picture of myself. And under those I drew one of me with her hairstyle.

No, as far as I could tell, we shared no traits.

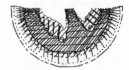

Fountain of Life

On Sunday the sculpture department was having an exhibit of fountains that had been built last semester. I figured if I arrived early, I'd be less likely to run into Nate and Clarissa.

The building was pretty empty when I got there. My feet echoed in the halls as I made my way to the exhibit room. I passed huge buckets of used clay. They were separated by color and wetness: the brittle dry red and gray clay stood in two buckets side by side, and the sloppy wet red and gray clay stood in two other buckets. The wet ones were labeled "Slip Buckets." I stuck my fingers in. It was cold and sludgy; the kind of stuff you liked to jump into as a kid.

I rinsed my hand in the hallway sink.

Aside from a monitor at the desk, the pieces in the exhibit, and a cheese-and-crackers table, the room was empty. I was glad to be able to look at the work in a quiet atmosphere, without tons of people milling about. The opening didn't officially start for another half hour.

Spaced evenly around the room were all sorts of fountains, but not the type that you see in parks. One fountain was a bunch of pipes and showerheads welded together. Another was simply a hose that snaked around the walls and ended at the doorway, pointing at your face as you entered. In one corner was a papier-mâché fire hydrant by Nate. None of the fountains actually had water coming out of them.

Except for one.

In the corner diagonally across from Nate's piece was a guy standing in a shallow metal tub — the kind in which women in Degas paintings bathe. The tub sat on top of a short white pedestal. The guy's body was entirely covered in black and white body paint, like a native warrior. He stood so still, I could hardly see him breathing. How is a painted naked guy a fountain? I wondered.

My question was soon answered when he started taking a leak. His "piece" was entitled *Fountain of Life*.

I looked up at him, and found that he was staring directly at me, accusingly, as if *I* was the one taking a naked piss in public. Our eyes remained locked until the stream trickled off.

People started flocking in.

I wondered how many times he could get himself to pee throughout the show.

I left before I could find out.

Rewind

I spent the afternoon in the library, curled up on a couch with *Ivan the Terrible*.

I thought back to the night Nate told me about his dad. Every time I remembered that story I thought, Nate and I are right for each other. If I could rewind time, I'd go back to that night and tell him why.

Then maybe his girlfriend wouldn't have come for a visit.

Maybe losing my virginity wouldn't have felt like such a mistake.

Icy snow skittered over the skylights. If you listened carefully, you could hear the flakes hitting the glass, like fingernails tapping a table.

Nine Motorcycles

My icicle feet were keeping me awake. I tried wrapping my sheets around them extra tight and pulling them into my pajama bottoms, but nothing helped. Socks would be the next step. But getting out of bed would mean making my entire body cold. That day I'd gone up the hill to Main Street and bought a CD of Itzhak Perlman playing Tchaikovsky's Violin Concerto in D. It was on now, coming to a close. I was giving myself until the end to get socks.

The orchestra hit its last chord, declaring my fate.

There was a knocking on the window. It didn't frighten me because I had almost expected it. I got the door for him, but didn't speak, and he climbed in beside me after removing everything except boxers.

"Whoa! Cold feet!" was all he said. He held them between his legs, slowly replenishing their warmth.

I lay as still as an ice statue.

"What're you thinking about?" he asked.

"I have a question for you," I said. "But I don't know how to say it."

Nate stroked my face. Like he was trying to memorize it. His eyes were fixed searchingly on mine. I shut my eyes, to try to keep him from drawing me in. We had some talking to do. But he rubbed his lips against mine. Back and forth and back again. Numbing my senses until I practically forgot I ever had anything to say to him, or that I even had a voice for that matter.

Before long we were rolling around in my sheets. I knew it was wrong. My head knew it was wrong. But I had already let him go this far. His skin felt so soft against mine that I didn't regret letting him undress me. He licked my neck and lips and kissed each of my eyelids. Stroking my hair, he lay his head down, resting his chin against my shoulder.

His breath was hot on my ear.

I'd been so mad at him I'd forgotten how good it was just to be touching him and to be touched.

Plus, he had brought protection, so there wasn't any logical reason to object. I mean, I was pretty into it, too. But when he pushed inside me, I couldn't wait for it to be over. The gentle touches, the kisses, they evaporated, and in their place was Nate pushing up and down. He was suddenly so heavy, I thought his weight might send me through the mattress. He moaned louder and louder and I hoped it would be over soon. Let him finish, I thought. Then we'll talk.

His nostrils were faintly whistling as we lay side by side.

Ask him something. Anything, I thought.

"Are you going to marry Clarissa?" is what came out. I have no idea where that came from. It must've been hiding in some dark crevice of my brain.

"I'm not getting married. I'm going to be a free spirit."

"Don't you want to have kids?"

"And spend the money I earn on them?"

"Mr. Generosity."

He turned on his side to face me. "I mean, it's going to be hard enough to make a living as an artist. I don't need a wife and kids to be money vacuums."

"But won't you feel like you're missing out on something?"

"Look," he said, "there's this thirty-seven-year-old guy I worked with last summer who owns nine motorcycles. He's not married, never had kids. But he loves those bikes, and he takes them to shows every chance he gets and rides them all over. He's probably the happiest man alive."

"I don't know about *that*," I said. "Maybe he's content."

"All you need is something to be passionate about. Like art."

"Or motorcycles," I added.

He kept inching closer to me, as if that would help to convince me of his argument. "Right, or motorcycles."

The stars on my ceiling were slowly dulling.

This was not the night to tell him why we were right for each other; it would have to wait.

To Be a Fish

I rolled over and tried to grab on to whatever sleep I could. I drifted in and out of consciousness, always hoping that this time I wouldn't open my eyes again before eight A.M. But when dusty dawn snuck its dull tired light through my blinds, I knew there wasn't much time left for me to get lucky with the Sandman.

I tried to get up with the impatient alarm, but Nate clung to me. Clamped me tight between his thighs.

"I have to go to class," I told him.

"Who cares about class?" He rolled me onto my back. Ran his palm up and down my body.

I wished I could give in to him. It almost seemed like I'd be stronger if I did. Rebel against academia. But I left and asked him to lock the door behind him. He didn't have to be at work until ten.

That day, Foundation was meeting at the nature lab to explore Ed's fish fantasy.

The nature lab was a well-lit room filled with live and dead fern and fauna for NECAD students to observe and draw. Some items could be borrowed from the lab, but most had to remain in the room at all times. Especially the hyperactive birds.

Ed wanted us to take a break from the technical accuracy of our previous assignments and explore patterns of movement. We were to choose a tank to observe, and with the drawing instrument of our choice, convey direction, line, and light. The first sketches shouldn't resemble anything recognizable. But in the final drawing we would incorporate some of our perspective training into these unstructured exercises.

"Begin not by showing me what the fish looks like, but how the fish *feels!*" Ed instructed. "Teach me what it is to *be* a fish!"

As if we knew.

"Unfortunately," he continued, "this facility is for public use, so we can't disrupt other visitors by playing music. But I am hoping that our friend Sam has brought his fish to listen to on headphones. And maybe if he is generous, he will share it with the rest of us!" He nodded expectantly at an eye-rolling Sam.

I had a feeling Sam wouldn't be that generous.

When Ed finished his speech, he stuck his face in front of a group of jumbo goldfish, the kind they keep in Chinese restaurants. He bulged his eyes and alternately sucked his cheeks in and puffed them out. I wouldn't have been surprised to see gills sprouting by his sideburns.

Ralph sucked in his laughter. Sam shot a look at me. My eyes held his gaze a few seconds before he blushed and directed his face downward.

I dragged a chair over to the largest tank of small, iridescent fish.

Now all I had to do was mentally become one of them.

Birds squawked. The tanks blew bubbles.

Ralph continued to survey the area, long after Sam and I settled on our spots. He moved methodically, peering carefully into each tank, as if the fish had perhaps changed into some other aquatic creatures since his last check. Maybe this time they would be salamanders. Or turtles. Bending his waist slightly, leaning close to the glass, his eyes tracked the fish like pendulums.

When he got back to the opposite side of my tank for the fifth round, I almost told him to make up his mind and sit down already. Every little detail raised huge questions and uncertainty for Ralph. There are bigger issues to be unsure about, I thought. Save it for something real.

At that moment, Ralph took a seat directly across from me. Of all the places he could've chosen, he had to sit precisely in my line of sight. There was no avoiding him.

All I had wanted that day was to be alone with my thoughts and the fish, to subtly sketch out my feelings. The old Ellie would've gone overboard, would've drawn bloated fish floating to the top of the tank. But the new Ellie was in control now, and she would show restraint; she had to find a way of masking her emotions, while still finding release.

The new way was much more difficult.

As I drew, I discovered that Ralph's position would actually work in my favor; his distorted features and darting irises would serve as a wonderful backdrop to those shimmering swimmers.

The LaLande Wetsuit

"I call it the LaLande Wetsuit," Ralph said from his seat.

We were back in the Garage and our sketches hung on the wall for an afternoon crit.

Ed planted his feet at shoulder's width and swayed from side to side, his brow furrowed. "Explain the diagrams, Ralph," he said. "Am I correct in assuming that the men in these pictures are wearing inflatable scuba gear?"

Ralph nodded. "That's pretty close. To be a fish would mean to be engulfed in wetness," he reasoned. "So I've designed apparel that would make a person literally feel what a fish is feeling."

He walked up to the wall, keys jingling, and pointed at the puffy suit. "It would be made of clear plastic and filled with water, giving the illusion that the person is submerged in liquid. You could even wear clothes under it and use it for work!" he exclaimed.

Sam slowly shook his head and rolled his eyes at me when Ralph wasn't looking.

Ralph continued. "In exploring this idea, I realized that this suit wouldn't make the wearer wet. So I came up with this model." He pointed at another diagram. "I added some squirt valves, to provide a constant spray. But then" — he looked at his feet — "then I saw my error: squirting simulates rain more than a large body of water. So this design really teaches us what it is to wear rain, not to be a fish." He sighed. "Sorry, but this was the closest I could come."

I know what it's like to wear rain, I thought. Go outside.

Although Sam came closer to producing what Ed had in mind, he also missed the mark. His fish were conveniently arranged in the shape of the Phish logo, bubbles and all. Although Ed didn't get the pop culture reference, he did know that Sam's fish had been schooled in the shape of themselves.

Ed paced in front of our results, eyes fixed on the floor.

"Both of your ideas, Sam and Ralph . . . both of them are quite inventive. I can't say I sense any movement, but I also can't deny that they are cute."

He stopped and turned to me. "Ellie, your fish are dynamic. They seem to be moving too fast for us even to catch a glimpse of them. The speed is exaggerated, but that is what makes the drawing interesting."

He paced again, this time in a circle around us.

"And Ellie, I'm glad to see that you've included Ralph — that is Ralph, isn't it?"

I nodded.

"I'm happy to see you've incorporated figurative elements into your work, because tomorrow" — he paused, taking a deep breath — "tomorrow we will start drawing the figure!"

Finally.

Electric Planning

Class got out early. I think Ed didn't want to have to come up with more comments for our work that day. I went to the computer lab. There hadn't been any mention of the e-mail I sent Nate last week. I had to write to him and tell him I took it back; it was presumptuous of me to think he was single. Maybe we should slow things down. Or just be friends.

Also, I was curious to see whether he ever left my bed that morning. I half expected someone else to be monitoring when I opened the door. Part of me wished it *would* be someone else.

But there he was at the front desk. Tongue pressed against the corner of his mouth. Eyes squinting at the screen. I walked up to him and he didn't notice I was there until I touched his shoulder. He jumped in surprise and quickly put the computer to sleep.

"Shouldn't you be in class, young lady?" he asked, recovering his composure.

"I got out early. I wanted to see if you woke up yet," I said. "What are you working on, anyway?"

"A project." He leaned back casually in the chair.

The screensaver stars soared toward the front of the screen.

"I've got some e-mailing to do," I said.

When I opened my account, I found a note from him.

> ellie yelinsky, let me tell you something. sex in general doesn't mean much to me. i see it as just a way of having fun. but you are changing that. yes, YOU. i've been with LOTS of girls. and most of them have been pretty damn CUTE (like you). but never have I met someone as genuine as you. i can tell when you say things, you really mean them. NO BULLSHITTING. you are something special. don't change.

Now what? I couldn't tell him, Sorry, I was only joking. Thanks for the compliment, but I'm not as great as you think I am.

The thing is, I really *had* meant what I'd written to him. But I didn't necessarily mean it right now. While thinking of an appropriate response, the bottom of my screen started flashing. Apparently Nathan Finerman wanted to "talk." I typed my way to the talk screen.

The awaiting message said:

> midnight. my house.

I wrote back:

> Sort of late, don't you think? School night.

He wrote:

come on, LIVE a little. i'm working on my project
until then. don't waste away your sexual peak.

I responded:

Okay, okay. Midnight.

Racing Dawn

I knew I shouldn't go. I knew it as I ran there, as I ran up to the
door and almost turned around. There was still a second left when
I could've gone back. Even after I rang the bell, I had time. But
there was a part of me rooted deep down, deeper than my brain
could reach with its relentless rationality, that wanted nothing
more than to see him, to lie with him, to wrap myself up in him.

It was that simple.

We hardly talked that night. For the first time, he seduced me
in the light. I saw that his entire back was tattooed to look like the
back side of a skeleton, each rib thinly outlined in permanent
black. He smelled like raw paint and turpentine, an odor that once
had been my own. I buried my nose in his thick hair and inhaled,
as if internalizing that smell would somehow identify me as a
painter again. But if given the opportunity to paint anything I
wished right now, I don't know what I would've chosen. I wanted

to create images portraying subtle human emotion, images that would speak to viewers for generations to come.

I followed the lines of his tattoo with my finger. I wondered if it was anatomically correct. This was the kind of thing I wanted to be learning in school.

"What are you doing?" he asked.

"Counting ribs."

"They're all there," he assured me. "Don't worry." He switched positions with me so that I was on my stomach and he massaged my back.

The radiator banged and hissed, banged and hissed.

"I've got to make sure yours are all here too," he whispered in my ear. He sat up so his legs were straddling my butt. Nate was heavy, but his weight was pleasant, holding me securely to the bed. He ran his fingers over each of my ribs from the spine out. Then he pounded on my back with the outer edge of his hands. For what felt like hours, he alternated between hard probing and squeezing, light tickly caresses, and scratching. I wished he would never stop.

By the time he finished with that I was so relaxed that *making love* didn't hurt much. For the first time, I opened my eyes during sex. We made eye contact and I didn't shut my lids again until his moaning started. I knew it would be over soon, but this time I wished it would last a little longer.

A great calm passed over him, leaving both his eyes and mouth closed.

I was almost asleep when he got up to turn off the lights, and I realized I couldn't stay there. The fact remained that he had a girlfriend, and I couldn't fool myself into thinking I was anything more than a lover to him. I began to get dressed.

"You look like you're getting ready to go out," he said with a laugh.

"I am," I said. "I'm going home. I'll sleep better there. I want to be well rested for my first day with models."

"It's a little late for that, don't you think?"

"I need to get at least *some* sleep."

"You can *sleep* with me, baby." He winked.

"Very funny," I said. "But I think I've had enough of that for tonight."

"Okay, but I can't see you again until Friday," he said. "I have to spend the rest of the week finishing this project."

He pulled me back onto his bed and flung my arm over his shoulder, forcing me to embrace him.

"Well, I'll see you Friday then," I said, wriggling out. I had to prove to him and to myself that I didn't *need* him. That I could be as casual about sex as he was.

I ran home, just in time to beat the eager dawn.

Figure Number One

Billy was in his terry-cloth robe and ready to go when we trekked in on Tuesday morning.

Ed started us out with gesture drawings. As with the fish, we were supposed to quickly convey what Billy was feeling, rather than what he looked like. To be honest, I preferred this option anyway, since Billy's body left much to be desired. If he had any muscles, his body fat provided just enough padding to hide them. Had he been blubbery, Billy would've been more fun to draw; at least then there would have been some shapes for us to focus on. The back of his thinning hair was pulled into a pug of a ponytail. His log legs hardly tapered toward his ankles.

Ed had Billy strike gestural poses on a modeling stand, a ten-by-seven-foot piece of wood on wheels. It helped to have the models raised a couple of feet off the ground, so we could see their entire bodies.

Billy seemed to think "gesture" meant stick your nonexistent hips out as far as you can in one direction for a minute at a time.

Ed coached him:

"Give us something a little more dramatic, Billy!"

Now in addition to the hips we got a forward stomach thrust.

After lunch Ed handed a mirror to each of us. "You guys are going to love this one!" he exclaimed. "Just wait till you hear your next assignment!"

We were waiting.

"In this next piece, Sam, Ralph, Ellie . . . in this next piece you will draw Billy in a long pose. And also, you will put yourself somewhere in the composition. Anywhere."

He paused for a reaction. Perhaps a standing ovation.

"So off you go! Take your mirror and find yourself in the drawing. Remember not to rush. You are in there somewhere, but only time will allow you to find yourself!"

Billy was much more at ease with the long pose, probably because he got to sit in a cushiony old armchair.

"Ed? Ed!" he called.

"What is it, Billy?"

"Do you mind if I hang my calendar so I can concentrate on it while I pose?" He waved his calendar in the air. The pictures were of baby animals dressed in doll clothes.

"That's fine, Billy. As usual. You know you don't have to ask anymore, after all these years."

Billy hung the calendar directly behind me. He was always staring just past my head. If he had been looking directly at me, it would've been less disconcerting.

Ralph later asked Billy, "What's the deal with the baby animals?"

"It helps me stay still and it gives me something to think about." Billy nodded his head as he talked, as if to compensate for our lack of empathy.

During a break, Billy paraded around the room in his robe, scrutinizing our drawings, telling each of us why they didn't look like him. The nose was too pointy, the eyebrows too bushy. What happened to the slight cleft in his chin, weren't we paying attention? None of us had any answers for him. Maybe if his face wasn't so nondescript, we wouldn't be having these difficulties.

Sam always stayed away from Billy when he wasn't posing.

By the end of the day, Billy had decided that my interpretation of his face was the best, and therefore blessed me with the gift of his baby animals calendar. Don't worry, he assured me, he had plenty of others at home. Piles, in fact. It would not be missed. He handed it over with a hopeful smile, as if this twenty-four-page booklet was supposed to inspire me to create masterpieces.

The Question

"Oh, a dragonfly!" Ralph exclaimed.

"Yes," Ed replied, "Tasha's dragonfly is always a big hit with new students!"

Tasha was a petite Indian woman in her late twenties with a tattoo of a dragonfly emerging delicately from her butt crack.

After putting her through a round of short gesture poses, Ed had Tasha lie on the modeling stand. He told her to roll back and forth so we could capture her movement. Round and round she went, dragonfly following with each turn. The dimples formed by her posterior superior iliac spines framed the dragonfly equally on either side.

"I hope this isn't too hard on you, Tasha!" Ed shouted.

"Oh, Ed," she called out between rotations, "only for you! Only for you!"

Tasha was much more graceful than Billy, possibly because she had once been an art student.

On our break, Tasha wrapped a satiny flowered sheet around her body and walked directly toward my easel. She pulled me aside and we sat on stools as she shared with me her artistic philosophy:

"I used to draw the figure, you know? But I realized that was pointless, because I wasn't making a statement, you know." Her irises were almost as dark as her pupils. I let my eyes blur, imagining that she just had two gigantic pupils. "So now, you know, I create what is meaningful to me, not what a teacher tells me to create. But this stuff is okay for now. You'll learn."

"What do you do now?" I asked.

Her pursed lips warned me that what was to escape them next would be dangerously profound.

"What I'm doing now is a musical study on mislabeled organic objects. For example, I place headphones on a tomato and play Bach."

She lowered her voice, as if to let me in on a well-kept secret.

"And, you know, a tomato is mislabeled because we categorize it as a *vegetable,* but in reality it's a *fruit,* you know?"

She touched my knee with her press-on claws.

"So, the question is: what exactly is the effect of Bach on a tomato?"

Yes, I thought, that's the question *exactly,* isn't it.

Perfect Proposal

Nate was sitting on my doorstep when I came home from dinner that night.

I ran up the steps; I had to pee badly.

"I thought you couldn't see me until Friday," I said. It was only Wednesday.

"Yeah, I know. I can't hang out for long." He stood up slowly. "I just needed someone to talk to."

We went inside.

"I don't usually confide in people," he said, collapsing on my bed. "But you're so easy to talk to. You're a good listener."

"What's going on?" I asked, taking a seat beside him. I crossed my legs.

"I talked to my mom last night," he said. "She's getting married. She only met the guy on a cruise three months ago. I've never met him. But I already know I can't stand him."

I recrossed my legs in the other direction and held them tightly together.

He continued. "I was thinking about it today, and I think I'd probably hate anyone she married. I know she dated people after

Dad died, but she never talked about it, so I pretended it never happened. Now that she's getting married, I feel like she's betraying Dad. And it all seems so irrelevant because I never even knew him."

I wanted to put my arms around him and pull him close, but I was afraid to move.

"Does this sound crazy and selfish?" he asked.

"No, not at all," I said. "It's more understandable than you think."

My bladder panged, but I held it.

"I feel like I'm such a whiner," he said. "I just needed to talk to someone."

"Maybe it'll help if I tell you a story," I said, my heart pounding faster.

"Okay," he said. "But after that I'm gonna get some painting done."

I squeezed my legs tighter.

"The story starts in the late sixties," I said, not sure how to begin. "I'll tell it to you the way my mom tells it."

He settled back against my pillow.

"My mom says life was different then. People didn't worry about things like AIDS."

Nate smiled. "Those were the days. Must've been a total blast."

"Maybe for some people."

"I would've been one of those people."

"*Well*, back then my mom used to go to concerts and leave with no clothes. Sometimes she'd go home with a stranger and not remember how she got there when she woke up."

"Been there," Nate said.

I rocked back and forth. Just get to the end of the story, I told myself.

"On weekends she'd go party-hopping and do whatever drugs and whatever men she could lay her hands on. She'd use birth control if it was around, otherwise she'd use the 'pull-out' method — which my sex ed teacher said isn't a method at all."

"You do what you've gotta do," Nate said.

I play-shoved him. That was the last movement my bladder could handle. I got up and ran. Well, it looked like more of a drunken trot than a run. But at least I made it to the bathroom in time.

"What's going on?" Nate called.

Then he heard the answer to his question.

"Niagara Falls!" He laughed. "I thought maybe I'd offended you!"

"No," I said over the sound of my never-ending pee, "I've just been holding this a long time!"

"You should've gone before!"

"But I didn't want to leave in the middle of what you were telling me!"

"Ellie, you're too good to me!"

When I came out, I lay on the bed with my legs finally at a comfortable distance.

"What a relief," I said.

"I bet," he said. "But what about the end of your story? It was just getting interesting."

"Where did I leave off?"

"The pull-out method."

"Oh, right. Anyway, my mom met my dad at one of those crazy

parties. They dated on and off for years and eventually he told her she was his only reason for living. He stopped seeing other people. He wanted her all to himself, but she wouldn't have it."

"Nobody owns anyone else," Nate said.

"Just be quiet and listen to the story."

"Okay, sorry." He sat up straight and folded his hands in his lap. "I'll be good."

"*Anyway*, my dad used to get mad at her for not being around to answer his phone calls late at night. She'd tell him they weren't married and he'd say, Well maybe we should be! His parents were pressuring him to settle down, which was fine by my dad because he'd already found his sweetheart. But his parents thought my mom was a slut. Not daughter-in-law material."

Nate grinned and put his hands behind his head. His biceps contracted inside his sleeves.

"My dad's parents sent him on a three-month cross-country trip, hoping he'd hunt down a new woman. But he didn't return with the girl of his dreams, because she'd been running around town sleeping with the hippies of Manhattan."

Nate laughed.

I took a deep breath. My heart was pounding hard again. "While he was gone she had gotten pregnant."

"It happens," Nate said. "The price of having fun."

"No, but listen," I said. "You have to be serious if you want me to tell the rest."

"Okay, I'm serious." He scrunched his face up into a "serious" look. "Go on."

"Well, my mom was six weeks into it already. She confided in my dad, her only trustworthy friend, that she didn't know what to do because she wanted to keep the baby, but how could she support it herself?"

"That was *you*?"

I nodded. "'I know what you should do,' he told her. She expected him to suggest abortion. Then, as my mom says, he held her face in his hands and, with a triumphant grin, he said, 'Marry me.'"

Not Knowing

"Why didn't you tell me before?" he asked, pulling me toward him by my armpits.

"I've never told anyone."

"But you knew I'd be able to relate," he said, squeezing me so hard I exhaled loudly.

"It was scary to tell you." I rested my head on his chest.

"Why scary?"

"Because what if I told you and you didn't react the way I wanted you to react?"

I heard his stomach gurgling against my ear. "How did you want me to react?"

"Just like you are."

My head rose and fell with each breath he took.

"I'm sorry," I said. "You have work to do. I kept you here longer than you meant to stay."

"No," he said. "Don't even think about that. I'm really glad you told me. I'll go to the studio in a little while. But I want to make sure you've said everything you want to say."

"My dad loves me like a real daughter," I said, making my eyes well up a little. "But at the same time —" I looked up at Nate and let a few tears sneak out. He pulled me on top of him and squeezed me tight. "At the same time, I just hate not knowing the real one." Nate wiped away my rolling tears with his thumb and smothered my face with kisses.

"I know," he whispered. "I know."

Still Alive with Violin

"Rose!" Ed shouted energetically.

"What!"

"Rose we have a special re —"

"What!"

"We have a special request for you today!"

"What's that!"

"We'd like for you to hold this violin and pretend you're playing it. Doesn't that sound like fun, Rose? Not your typical modeling job!"

There was nothing innately wrong with the concept, except that

Rose couldn't have been younger than 150. She was practically deaf, and I doubt she could hear herself think, let alone tune a musical instrument.

Ed presented the saggy, naked Rose with one of those scuffed-up violins from our still-life assignment and she yelled, "Oh, I used to play the fiddle! Hard to believe, ain't it?"

Within about twenty minutes of posing, Rose began to fall asleep. No, she was dying. Dying slowly with a wrecked violin in her drooping arms. And to top it all off, Ed played the Tchaikovsky violin concerto tape.

"Just like the real thing, right Ellie?" he said, pointing from Rose to the boom box and back again.

"What!"

"Never mind, Rose!" Ed said, rushing up to the modeling stand.

"What!"

"I said, Never mind, it's okay, just go back to posing!" he shouted, standing about a foot away from her.

Ed gave Rose more frequent breaks than the other models to keep her from completely conking out.

At the first break Rose went to her pocketbook and whipped out proof of her youth in a Ziploc bag: snapshots of herself outdoors, beautiful and unwrinkled.

"Come look, kiddies! You won't believe your eyes!" The three of us gathered around, passing the pictures to one another. Up close I saw that now she was missing most of her teeth.

"You were very beautiful, Rose," Ralph said.

"What!"

Ed came to the rescue. "Ralph was just noting what a knockout you are in these pictures, Rose!"

Sam turned to me so that no one else could see and gave the pictures the thumbs up sign, nodding slowly. I squinted at him. I couldn't believe Mr. Eye Roller was making a joke. His face flushed red and he quickly looked away.

"Oh, yes!" Rose yelled. "The men were quite taken with me! And can you believe I once played the fiddle?" she asked again.

Yes, it was hard to believe that Rose had once played the violin. It was a stretch to imagine her arthritic fingers moving at their own will. But it was even harder to believe she was still alive. And that she took off her clothes for a living.

"You look so natural with that violin, Rose!" Ed would call out from time to time, trying to keep her from collapsing in her chair. He was right; what could be more natural than a naked old lady supporting a beaten violin between her thin layered chin and misshapen hand?

Upon hearing Ed's voice Rose would wake with a start. Realizing she had an instrument in her grasp, she'd pluck haphazardly at the miserably out of tune strings, accompanied by a sunken grin.

The Billy Assignments

On Friday Ed critiqued the Billy assignments. I had drawn myself peeking through a slightly ajar doorway behind Billy. The expression on my face was one of disgust, as if I had walked into my living room only to find my old overweight uncle with no clothes in Dad's armchair.

Ralph's drawing also depicted him standing behind Billy, but he held two fingers in a V shape over the naked guy's head. Although I can't say I thought his idea was great, I enjoyed imagining Ralph standing in front of the mirror with his two fingers extended for hours, laughing to himself about his little joke.

Sam had put himself in a seat beside Billy, facing forward and smoking a joint.

"Fantastic!" Ed shouted. "Utterly fantastic!"

My head was bobbing again from lack of sleep. Maybe if Ed gave us some real criticism, I'd have an easier time staying awake.

"These drawings all say something, don't you think? I gave you each the same assignment and you all came up with something different."

"Do you ever have anything negative to say about student work?" Ralph asked.

That woke me up.

"Interesting question, Ralph," Ed said. "Not very often! On occasion I'll get a student who doesn't want to do the work I assign. For example, they might come in and do a performance rather than actually make a drawing. I have very little patience for that!"

"What do you mean, a performance?" Ralph asked.

Sam shot me an uh-oh look.

"Well, what I mean, Ralph, is imagine that our friend Sam had come in here and lit up a joint in front of our class. That is a joint, isn't it, Sam? Not a cigarette?"

Sam's Adam's apple, his thyroid cartilage, bounced as he gulped. He nodded, pulling his cap forward.

"So imagine, Ralph, that Sam had come in here and smoked up instead of creating this drawing."

"Yeah, and why is that worse than drawing it? This doesn't seem like the kind of picture a teacher would approve of."

Another look from Sam.

"It's not that I approve of smoking, Ralph," Ed answered. "It's just more powerful to see Sam's interpretation of himself than to simply see him sitting in front of us. If you can believe it, in this context, there's more depth to the two-dimensional Sam than to the three-dimensional Sam! When Sam comes to class every day, he only shows us what he wants us to see of his personality. But here in this picture, Sam looks more mysterious. As if he's thinking thoughts he would never tell us!"

"Like what?" asked Ralph.

"Well, I'm not going to venture to guess because it's not my place to do so," Ed said. "But it is interesting to speculate, isn't it?"

"I've never thought about it that way," Ralph said.

Neither had I. I sure hoped there was more going on in Sam's mind than it seemed. Pot, Phish, and doughnuts would get boring real fast.

As the conversation slipped back to Ed's usual praising banter, I slid back into sleepy mode. I could've easily gone straight home after class and slept soundly into the morning.

But I was curious to see how Nate's "project" had worked out.

Out-of-Class Model

That night I saw the completed piece at Nate's house. He'd cleared a path in the fire hydrant mess from the door to the new painting. I tried not to look at the wall covered with girls as I traipsed through. They were probably all ex-girlfriends and I didn't want to know what they looked like.

He was a better painter than I'd expected, considering the simplicity of his fire hydrants. I recognized the model. She was wearing a tight pink tank-top and black leggings, which were not entirely flattering to her otherwise voluptuous body. I was sure Ralph wouldn't approve of her style.

"I think I've seen that model on campus," I said. "She looks really familiar."

"She's no model," Nate said, and laughed. "You've seen her because she's a student. Maura Bustier. She's in my class."

"Oh," I said. "Is that the assignment? To paint a classmate?"

"No, just anything from life. But what better way is there to improve your figure painting skills than to paint the figure?"

"Did she paint you, too?"

"She did a still life," he said. "Wine bottle and grapes. *Bo*-ring."

I wondered if she had kept her clothes on for her entire visit with Nate.

I sure didn't.

Forever Influenced

Nate was knocking.

I'd made a point of not staying over last night, but I'd left late. On my way home, I decided that it was okay with me if he ever wanted to stay here. I wouldn't object. But if I slept at his place, I'd be allowing him to have too much control over me.

It was only around three when he arrived that afternoon, but it was dark enough outside for it to be almost evening. The sky was like a global down comforter. Nate sat me facing him in his lap on my bed and kneaded my head.

"Is that a new drawing?" he asked, pointing to the one I had done of Billy and myself. It was hanging on the wall across from my bed.

"Yeah, that was one of my assignments last week," I said. "Put yourself in the picture."

"What a great idea!" he said, pressing harder on my scalp. "And that's a great drawing. You're really talented." He lifted my chin with his other hand so he could look me in the eye.

I thanked him.

He guided my face to his with his fingers and kissed me long and slow. He dragged his teeth over my lower lip and bit it just to the point of hurting.

"Do that more," I said.

"You like the biting?" he asked, with his lips still against mine.

"Yeah," I said. "It's weird how it hurts, but still feels really good."

Pretty soon we were naked under the covers. It was perfect weather to be in bed with someone: cold and dark with weighty snow clouds. When we were done *making love,* I pulled up my shades so we could stare at the sky upside down through my window bars.

"What if you shoveled those clouds away," I wondered aloud. "Would there be a bright blue sky behind them?"

"No," he said, "if you tried to move any of that stuff out of the way, more would move right over and cover up the gap."

Before we fell asleep he wrapped my arm around his waist from behind like a seat belt. He secured my hand in one place with his own, kept me buckled in, and asked me about my past sex life.

"You're it," I told him.

"No way!" he said. "I would never have known! You're a natural." He rolled over, setting me free.

After a short silence, he said in a softer tone, "You know, that makes me feel really special. That I'm your first. Your style will forever be influenced by me."

Acting Too Queer

The 2-D segment had begun, and the three of us were hard at work in the Garage at night. Ed had told us to get an object from the nature lab and to make a magnified drawing of it with a handmade tool or found object.

I was doing a pinecone with pine needles and ink. Ralph was doing a feather with a feather and ink. And Sam was busy smoking his hand-rolled cigarettes so he could use the ashes with a stump made from folded rolling papers. His object was a conch shell. Every once in a while he'd hold it to his ear and zone out. Maybe the shell was telling him how to be a better draftsman.

"Sam, why do you smoke?" Ralph asked.

Sam glared at Ralph. "It makes me feel good."

"I didn't mean to offend you," Ralph said. "It's bad for you, is all."

"I want to die young," Sam said. "I don't want to end up like that model Rose."

For a while we all kept quiet. Our found objects scratched against paper.

"Can I talk to you guys about something?" Ralph asked.

"What?" I knew he would keep going whether we said he could or not.

"Now, you have to promise not to laugh."

"Okay," I said.

"Both of you," he said, looking at Sam.

"Sure," Sam said.

"I'm starting to worry that I'm acting too queer."

"In what way?" I asked, putting down my pinecone.

"I mean, I might as well be wearing a sign that says, HEY NECAD, I'M HOT FOR GUYS! I mean, I love show tunes, I giggle like a schoolgirl, I even *walk* like I'm gay! But you know what? I can't help it!"

He looked back and forth from me to Sam. Sam to me.

"Can't a guy be an apparel designer without being labeled a fag?"

"Well, are you?" Sam asked.

"As a matter of fact, I am, but that's beside the point. I want people to think Apparel first; Queer second. Not the other way around."

"Maybe if you dressed differently," I suggested.

"I dress this way so people know I'm serious about fashion!"

He started pacing around us, flinging dramatic gestures as he spoke.

"When girls hang out with me, all they want to do is go guy-watching. And I mean, that's fun, it's *a lot* of fun, but none of them ever want to talk about what I *really* love! And who will talk to you about clothing if not girls?"

"Maybe other gay guys," I said.

"But that's exactly what I want to avoid!" He threw his arms in the air. "Can't you see that's just perpetuating the stereotype?"

He had gotten so caught up in his misery that he'd forgotten the ink-loaded feather in his hand. He looked down and noticed that in his last sweeping gesture he had swung a black stain straight across his baby blue polyester cowboy shirt.

"My God," he cried, "my new shirt!"

The Heart of Painting

"So what's that scar from?" I touched it lightly.

"Vietnam," he said.

"Right," I said. "Did you also pick up your sense of humor there?"

"Yeah." He smirked.

"Where's it really from?"

"I got it in San Francisco."

"How?" I brushed his hair back from his forehead and kissed the white outline on his jaw.

"Fine, I'll tell you," he said, "but nobody here knows about this."

"Who am I going to tell?" I asked, massaging his scalp. "Besides, I've told you my biggest secret." I let my fingers get lost in massive tufts of thick hair.

"I was a painting major at the Art Institute," he began.

The window in front of the bars was foggy from our *love* making.

"Freshman year, my goal was to be the best painter at school."

I raised an eyebrow.

"I know it sounds cocky," he said, "but people were painting bullshit. One guy made a five-by-five-foot canvas covered with meticulously painted Band-Aids. They were supposed to portray his attempt to cover up his pain. People would talk about that garbage for hours, but none of it had anything to do with skill."

He turned on his side, propping his head up with his hand.

"I wanted to get to the heart of what painting was all about," he told me.

He lay back down.

"I churned out a ton of self-portraits, until I could produce my likeness easily. When I got tired of that, I added props. I found costumes in thrift stores. I posed as a king, as a knight, as the Devil."

The fog on the window was evaporating. I pressed the side of my fist on the glass, and topped the imprint with five dots.

"A baby foot!" Nate said, hugging me. "You do the cutest things."

"Keep talking."

"Right. What was I saying? Oh yeah. I got tired of painting myself. Plus, I really wanted to be painting women. I hired models. During the first semester, I had one model come each week. By the second semester I was using two or three models at a time. Or sometimes I would hire one model to stand in a few different poses, and I'd integrate them into the same painting. I built my canvases bigger and bigger until they were practically the same height as the studio wall."

He paused, scrunching his eyebrows.

"All the other kids thought I was a showoff."

I ran my finger up and down his sternum. I liked the slight angle where the manubrium met the gladiolus.

"But anyway, one day I was on a ladder, setting the lights back to the same angles they were at for the last session. The model was in place on one side of me, and on the other side I was holding my huge painting. With my free hand I reached to turn the light."

He looked up at the window. "Hey, the baby foot's almost gone!"

We watched the fog around the toes evaporate.

"We'll have to find a way to fog that window up again so you can make another!" he said, tickling me.

"Stop!" I laughed, prying his fingers from my sides. "So you reached to turn the light . . ."

"Oh, right!" His hands relaxed. "And that's when I forgot something crucial: I forgot that when lightbulbs are on, they're hot. As soon as I touched it I lost my balance. The ladder tipped so slowly there seemed to be enough time to stop it, to push it back in place.

I lost my grip, so I clung to the painting to keep from shooting straight down. But of course the painting couldn't hold me up. As it toppled over, I let go and my face headed directly toward the stretcher bars. I tucked my head in, so only my jaw grazed the center stretcher. I could hear everything crashing around me. The ladder, a table, buckets of water, glass jars."

"Wow, sounds like you were lucky if that's the worst that happened."

"Well, I broke my leg. I guess my painting was more damaged than I was. I fell right through the canvas. I ripped a hole in the model's chest. And those were some melons," he said wistfully.

The entire baby foot had disappeared, swept up by the fog.

"How long before you recovered?"

"I was on crutches for a month, but I never got over it emotionally. Everyone knew what had happened. They saw this as their opportunity to get back at me for being such a painting snob. In bathroom stalls I found pictures of my face with lightbulbs over my head. I became known as Lightbulb Boy. One of the printmaking majors silkscreened T-shirts with a lightbulb on the front and a naked woman on the back. I knew I had to get out of there when I saw those shirts. I had to start over in a new place, with a new major."

"Why sculpture?"

"Sculpture is more direct. You imagine an object and you make it. Painting involves layer upon layer of color and revisions. I've always wanted my paintings to look real, to tell a story or to show a personality. I still love to paint, but I can get my ideas out quicker in three dimensions."

He sighed and rolled onto his back once more.

"Or at least that's what I tell myself," he said. "I don't know. Maybe what happened in California was so traumatic that I don't want to get seriously involved with painting again."

"Why are you painting now?"

"To get the ladies." He grinned, gauging my reaction.

I shoved him toward the wall.

"I missed it," he said, laughing. "I wanted to see if I still really loved it, once I'd taken a break."

"Maybe you should throw your heart back into it while you have the chance."

"You're right," he said. "I really should."

Seeing Spots

We were standing in the Garage driveway, huddled around a pile of construction paper. An orange page was on top.

"Stare at the orange. Stare at it, Ralph. Ellie. Sam. Don't move your eyes. I know you have to blink, but try not to," Ed commanded.

Then he removed the orange sheet, leaving a white one on top.

"Now look at the white! What color do you see? What color, Ellie?" He scampered over to me.

"Blue," I said.

"Exactly. You see blue! And do you know why? Do you know, Sam?"

Sam looked at him, but didn't answer, cap shading his eyes.

"The reason, Sam, is because blue and orange are complementary colors! They are opposites on the color wheel! When you look at a color for a long time, your eye produces an afterimage! But the afterimage isn't really there! It's an optical effect!"

Ed shuffled through the pile of papers, searching madly.

"Ah, perfect. Perfect, perfect! Okay, now I want you to do the very same thing you just did." He laid a small green piece over a large red piece. "Ready . . . begin! Stare at the colors! Make sure you're looking at both colors!"

We stared.

"Do you see how the colors are vibrating? This is what happens when two complementary colors are beside one another! Boy, is that crazy, or what? Here we have two inanimate objects, but my eyes are picking up movement! Vibrations!"

Ed rubbed his eyes in disbelief.

"Okay, you can stop staring," he said, putting the white on top once more.

This time the red and green had traded places.

"Ed, isn't this bad for our eyes?" Ralph asked.

"No. No, Ralph. Not at all. On the contrary. This is great training for your eyes. It will help your color sense significantly."

"I mean, all you're doing is making us see spots. Couldn't you teach us color theory without making us see spots?"

"I suppose so, Ralph. But I find that this demonstration is a great introduction for first-year students. And I have such fun every time I teach it!"

He grabbed Ralph by the sleeve.

"Ralph! Just look at your shirt! It doesn't get any better than this!" It was purple with a yellow paisley print.

Ed focused on the fabric. Then he turned to the white paper.

"Holy bazungas! You guys should check this out! That is great! Those yellow spots are purple now! Try it, Ellie. Try it, Sam. And Ralph, if you can get a good enough angle on that shirt, you try it too! It would be a shame for you to miss such a textbook example!"

Meat Market Girl

While I was walking down Artist's Row Friday morning, Nate whooshed by with a fresh painting about half his size.

"Can't talk. I'm in a rush!" he yelled, as if I couldn't tell. "Call me tonight!"

The canvas bumped against his back as he ran. It was another girl. But this beauty was buck-naked. Or "nude," as they say in art school.

No, if it's a classmate, she's buck-naked.

I knew who it was. Sloane Boocock, who had stood behind me in the new ID line. She'd lost her old one at the Artist's Ball. Her voice was high-pitched, as if only her body had made it through puberty. She wore a clingy cropped sweater beneath her unzipped coat.

"This school is a meat market," she'd warned me, pointer finger extended. "Don't let 'em fool you. They're all assholes."

Maybe he *was* just painting them. Art students must pose for each other all the time. Besides, I wasn't his girlfriend anyway.

She's the one who should be bothered by all this.

A Big Stink

I had to go bad. And I don't mean number one. I made a run for the dining hall.

There was only one unclogged stall left and I got to it just in time. As I finally began to relax, two chatty girls came in. I hoped they wouldn't be waiting for my seat. Luckily, it seemed they were only making a quick appearance-check. Through the crack in the door I could see them examining their pores.

They were in the middle of an animated debate.

"I *told* you I never posed for that scumsucking bastard of a shit!" one of them said.

"Well, neither did I! *You* at least got to wear clothes!" the other one answered in a little girl's voice. Her breasts looked like they wanted to jump out of her low-cut stretch shirt.

"But they weren't *my* clothes? I never wear anything that tight?

And are my breasts really that big? And my thighs? I don't think so?" Almost everything this one said sounded like a question.

I squinted through the door. It was them all right.

"No, I'm sure he exaggerated," Sloane said. "His only guide for your proportions was his imagination!"

"Whatever. He could've at least given me something flattering to wear? A robe would have been better? Or even a bathing suit?" Poor Maura; she was always asking questions that would never be answered.

"I just can't believe Fritz didn't say anything!" Sloane ranted. "It's like he actually thinks I took my clothes off for a picture my entire class would crit!"

"Leggings and a bodysuit are just as bad?" Maura's voice trailed off with the groaning door.

As they stomped away in platform-shoe unison, one of them flipped the light switch.

Unfortunately, my business in the ladies room was not entirely finished.

As soon as I was done, my quest for the truth began.

That Scumsucking Bastard of a Shit

"You didn't *really* paint them, did you?" I asked right away.

"Yes I did. You can see the paintings for yourself." He pointed at the canvases of Maura and Sloane leaning against his wall. He had pushed aside some fire hydrants to display his new work.

"Of course I see them," I said, "but did they really pose for you?"

"Well, it depends on what you mean. Yes, they posed. But not specifically for me."

Nate told me about his scheme. He'd been superimposing headshots from the Freshman Face Book on various magazine model bodies with Photoshop. Working at the computer lab allowed him ample time to perfect the image before transferring it to canvas. His goal was to do a portrait of every girl in the class alphabetically. There were five; exactly enough for one per week. He already had two down.

Nate thought next week was going to be tough, though. Melinda Cassidy was, as he said, a "gigantress." He didn't want to make her uncomfortable. But skipping over her would be even more insulting. Plus, Melinda was most likely of all the girls to call his bluff.

He was very interested in hearing about Maura and Sloane's outrage, and made me repeat several times what they'd called him.

"A scummy bastard son of a bitch?" He laughed as he paced around the creaking floor.

"No, a scumsucking bastard of a shit."

"What the hell does *that* mean?"

"I don't know. I guess they don't like you."

"Well, they shouldn't. But I'll bet you anything they let me get away with this."

Wall of Girls

After learning the truth from Nate, I stayed at his place for a pasta dinner. He cooked a pot of fusilli — long twisty macaroni that looks like curly hair. In my haste to see him, I'd forgotten to eat.

I sat on his bed while he cooked.

I turned to face the wall of girls, the wall that I'd tried to avoid looking at every time I was there. Knowing about Nate's scheme made me feel braver.

Then I realized that the wall wasn't a wall of *girls;* it was a wall of *girl!* They were all Clarissa, in different styles. It was like a lineup of Barbies. Punk Rock Clarissa, Churchgoing Clarissa, Math Nerd Clarissa, Cowgirl Clarissa. Her hair varied in length and color. Her clothes went from prudish to risqué, frilly to clean-cut. There had to be at least twenty versions.

"Nate!" I cried. "These pictures are all of Clarissa!"

"Yeah, you didn't know that?"

Boiling water sizzled over the top of the pot. The sound blended with the radiator's hiss.

"I thought they were all different women! I thought they were all the women you'd slept with!"

He laughed. "I guess you could say that. I mean, I do feel like I'm sleeping with a different woman almost every time I see her."

"How does she feel about that?"

"I think that's partly why she does it," he said. "To keep things interesting."

"Would things be boring if she always looked the same?"

"It takes a lot to keep the flame burning, if you know what I mean."

"I guess so," I mumbled.

Part of me felt less threatened, knowing they were all Clarissa. But in a way I felt sorry for her.

The radiator switched from hissing to banging and steaming. It had gotten so hot that I was breaking a sweat. I went over to the radiator to turn it down. The banging was loud near my ears. I couldn't find a knob.

"How do you lower the heat?" I called to Nate in the kitchen.

"You can't! The landlord controls it. It's included in the rent!"

We hung out for a while after dinner. I didn't stay past ten. He tried to coax me into sleeping over, but I said it was too hot in there and I wouldn't be able to sleep through the radiator noises. He walked me down the path to the road, where he kissed me goodnight and said, "Come on, don't you think it would be better if you stayed? It's freezing out here."

"No," I said, "it'll be better if I go home."

Or better yet, I thought, if you didn't make me feel like I needed to go home.

"Are you gonna run again?"

"How did you know I ran?"

"I watch you from the window every time you leave. You look so cute bounding down the path."

"I didn't know you watched me." I was blushing.

"Why do you run, anyway?"

"I run to get a head start on the guy who's chasing me."

He laughed.

I laughed.

Then I ran.

It All Makes Sense

I was glad to get a good night's sleep because I was able to wake up early in the morning and go to the NECAD museum to draw.

I planted myself in front of their biggest sculpture, Rodin's *Hand of God*. Not the original sculpture, but a plaster cast. I figured it would be a good hand study.

Apparently, I had good taste; a guy circled the piece slowly, followed by a girl in a Harvard sweatshirt. He wore thick black retro glasses and a soiled post office jacket.

"So profound," he mumbled.

"What?" she said.

"Sooooo profound," he answered, a few decibels louder.

"What do you mean?"

"This man," he said, pointing at the identification plaque, "was so brilliant. Sooooo brilliant."

She cocked her head sideways at the sculpture, then straightened it.

"In what way?" she asked.

"So there's this huge hand, right? And it's the hand of God, obviously, according to the title. So we know that's Adam and Eve he's scooping out of the clay, right?"

"Right," she said tentatively.

"But it doesn't end there. It's not *merely* the hand of God. That would be too simple. Do you see where I'm going with this?"

"Um, I think so," she said.

"Who else's hand is it?"

"The sculpture's?"

"Close." He laughed. "It's the hand of the sculpt*or*. The artist. The art*iste*." He paused, absorbing the profundity of his last words. "While God is building his human creation out of clay, Rodin is building this sculpture out of the very same medium. He, in effect, has control over God's creation and God's hand. It's as if the artist *is* God, is more powerful than God."

"More powerful than *God*?" she interrupted.

"Well, superhuman, at least," he concluded, scratching his stubble.

"Wow," she said, "I never really *get* art when I look at it. But when someone explains it to me, it's like it all makes sense."

The Melinda Cassidy Problem

I was listening to Tchaikovsky's violin concerto when Nate knocked on my window. He was holding a big hardcover book.

When he came in he threw the book on my bed. Then he ran to the kitchen and grabbed the champagne bottle my dad had given me.

"We have reason to celebrate," he said, and pulled me by the hand out to the winding hallway, then through the rickety back door. He put the bottle on the ground and lifted me like I was a child and ran across slabs of slate to the center of the patio. He whirled me around before placing me in a long lawn chair. My body sunk into the plastic strips.

He got the bottle and shook it up and down.

"What's this all about?" I asked.

"The Melinda Cassidy Problem. I've found a solution." He unwrapped the bottle and popped the top, aiming it in the air so it sprayed us from above. We took turns drinking the remainder of the bottle's contents and went inside to rinse off.

This wasn't how I'd imagined my dad's champagne would be used. I thought it would be for the end of Wintersession, or the end of a long project. Not the Melinda Cassidy Problem.

In the steamy heat of the shower Nate told me his plan.

Instead of painting each girl in his class, he would continue to work only on Sloane Boocock. Would she be able to stand seeing three more Natesque paintings of herself without saying anything? Nate's guess was, Yes, she would put up with it. She was too much of a wimp to actually confront him. Meanwhile, he would enjoy watching her fume.

This week he'd paint her lying on a bed, in a style reminiscent of Manet's *Olympia*. Throw a little art history into the mix, he said. That's why he'd borrowed a Manet book from the library. He'd show me the picture when we got out of the shower.

"So what do you think?" he asked.

"Sounds *brilliant*."

"That didn't sound convincing."

"No, it's a good plan." Control the sarcasm, I told myself.

"What's wrong?"

"Nothing," I said. "I guess I'm just tired or something."

I kept picturing his wall of Clarissas, and wondered if he'd start a new wall for Sloane. He kissed me long and hard. My face backed away as his lips pressed against mine.

"Let's get out of here," he said, hugging me so tight that there was suction between our bodies. "Do you happen to know a place where a guy can find a warm bed and a hot woman round these parts?"

I rested the knob on cold before shutting off the spray.

"What did you have to do that for!" he said as the water hit his back.

"I like the shock of the temperature change."

I followed his lead to the land of dryness.

Psychedelia

I was going to do a good job on this color project, even if it meant staying in the Garage until Ed fluttered in the next morning. And anyway, Nate had warned me that he'd have to work on his homework for the rest of the week. I wondered if he'd actually be able to pull off *Sloanolympia*. Part of me wanted it to turn out badly.

It was around ten P.M., and Ralph must've finished early because it was just me and Sam. And Sam's empty Dunkin' Donuts bag.

A small tinny rhythmic sound escaped through Sam's headphones.

Our new 2-D assignment was to take our magnified drawings and redo them in complementary colors with gouache. The final images had to express an emotion.

I asked Sam what his was.

"Psychedelic," he said, removing his headphones.

Blue and orange ovals and elongated triangles spiraled around Sam's paper.

It seemed to me that "psychedelic" wasn't an emotion. Or at least not what Ed had in mind. But I had to hand it to him; I couldn't think of a more appropriate word to describe his painting.

"Mine's claustrophobia," I told him. It was embarrassing to say out loud; I'd always thought that art should speak for itself.

I had set it up so the center segments of the pinecone were red, while the outer ones were green.

"Cool," he said, turning his piece so he could view it from different angles.

"You think so?"

"Sure. Just about any state of mind that ends with 'ia' is cool. Claustrophobia, paranoia," he said, sneaking a glance at me from under his droopy hat, "psychedelia."

"That's not a state of mind, is it?"

"Yeah." He let out a goofy chuckle. "No. Maybe not, but at least it sounds cool."

Bowling Ball

The next day I was late for dinner, so I went to the Grind. The difference between the Grind and the dining hall is that the dining hall at least offers you the choice of being healthy; your only choice at the Grind is deep-fried chicken-filled grease.

I sat in my bouncy red booth, chowing on chicken fingers and fries, sketching after-hours diners. The green walls were lit by incandescent bulbs behind hubcaps.

Behind me sat a couple of girls, heavily involved in a hushed conversation. They leaned close over the Formica table. If I sat all the way back against my seat, I could hear bits of what they were saying.

"No way!" and "Then what?" was all I heard at first. But after a while they weren't so careful to keep quiet. From my strategic position, everything was clear with minimal ear straining.

"What did it feel like?" one of them asked.

"It was reeeeeally good," the other said.

"Really good is not an answer. You know me. I need details. What did it feel like?"

"It was like . . . a bowling ball!"

"What do you mean, a bowling ball?" The way she was giggling I knew she could only be talking about one thing.

"I mean, it was huge. And it came bursting out from within me like a bowling ball hitting all the pins at full speed."

"Wow, no one's ever given it to me that good."

A bowling ball.

Nothing I'd experienced with Nate had anything to do with any type of ball, let alone a bowling ball. If the second girl had never had it as good as a bowling ball, maybe she'd at least had it as good as a baseball or tennis ball. Perhaps even golf or Ping-Pong.

I wondered if Nate would understand. I didn't plan on asking him, though.

He might discover I'm not such a natural after all.

Business at Home

Ed stood on the modeling stand and shouted, "Everybody! I have an announcement! Are you ready?"

"Yes," I said. I was the only one to answer.

"Ralph, Sam, are you ready, too?"

"Yes, Ed," Ralph said lazily.

"Uh-huh." Sam raised the brim of his cap just enough to see Ed.

"Well, I guess we're all ready then! First of all, I'm sorry to do this, but I'm going to have to start my weekend early today. I'll be leaving shortly to take care of some business at home."

The three of us shot excited looks at each other.

"I'm glad to see you'll miss me!" he shouted. "Since I won't be here, I want you to start thinking about your next assignment. Get some sketches together in the next couple of days and I'll lecture on Monday. Everybody, we have reached the final phase of our Foundation fun! Do you know what that means?"

"Two more weeks?" Ralph guessed.

"One more try!" Ed shouted.

"Three-D?" I asked.

"And the refrigerator goes to Ellie Yelinsky!" Ed shouted in his game-show-host voice. "Now, for your final projects, I want you to create a three-dimensional space. But this space has to be in the shape of an object that is not usually considered a space! Doesn't that sound like a challenge?"

"So, you mean we can't make a cave?" Ralph asked.

"You've got it, Ralph!"

"Can it be something from nature?"

"Ralph, as long as you don't normally think of it as a space, you can make it!"

"Can it be big?" Ralph asked.

"It's all up to you!" Ed shouted. "Just bring me sketches next week and I'll discuss them with you individually on Monday!"

He hopped down off the modeling stand.

"Okay, unless anybody else has questions, I'll be going! Like I said before, I'm terribly terribly sorry to be taking time away from you. I'll stay after class next week if anybody needs my assistance."

He scurried around, collecting his coat, portfolio case, and bag of supplies, and zipped out the door.

"So long, Ellie! So long, Sam! So long, Ralph! See you next week!" he shouted.

"Bye," we said in unison.

"That guy's actually starting to grow on me," Ralph said.

"What do you think he has to do?" I asked.

"Maybe there's something wrong with his wife," Ralph said.

"Is he married?" I asked.

"I don't know," Ralph said.

"Do you think he's gay?"

"Absolutely not," Ralph said. "My gaydar hasn't picked up anything."

"Do you think he even has a girlfriend?"

"No way," Sam said.

"Why not?" I asked. "You said that so emphatically."

"You think any girl could put up with that much energy?"

Ralph and I laughed.

"Yeah," Ralph said, "I can see it. Sure, honey, I'll go to bed with you, but only if you hold still for five minutes."

"Not that I even *want* to picture that," I said, "but I can't imagine he lies down to sleep, let alone to sleep *with* someone!"

"No kidding," said Ralph, in hysterics. "He'd wear *me* out!"

A Real Shocker

That night I asked Nate how the crit went.

We stood in the center of his room, looking at his paintings. The fire hydrants had been pushed against the walls. As usual, there was a party going on inside his radiator.

Nate said that his teacher, Fritz, had expressed his admiration for both Nate's and Sloane's maturity in the matter, and for acting so professional. The Manet reference was impressive. He even complimented Sloane on her pose.

Instead of protesting that she'd had nothing to do with it,

Sloane thanked him and said she'd been working on it. Posing makes her identify better with models in class.

"Can you believe the nerve of that ho?" Nate demanded, kicking a fire hydrant head into the kitchen. "She shouldn't get credit for my stunt! Plus, I think she's actually beginning to like the attention! I'll have to throw in a real shocker next time."

I couldn't take my eyes off a picture on his wall of him and Clarissa with her half-and-half hairdo.

I wanted to ask him if Clarissa knew about this project. If she knew about me. What she thought about the situation, if she did.

But the questions couldn't escape my lips.

I felt as if right outside my mouth was one of those sharp toothy devices that they have on the ground at parking garage booths. You can drive over them, but if you back up, your tires pop. That's what would've happened to my words; once they came out they would have to keep rolling forward.

We both stood there, staring at his two paintings of Sloane.

Ask him now, I thought. Now, while we're not in bed.

But I didn't. Pretending that I didn't have questions, that I didn't care if I was just another fling for him, was easier than dealing with a direct answer. Because hearing his answer might mean letting go of a warm body in the winter, of fingers in my hair, of a rib cage tattoo. And the thrill of running at night, knowing that someone in the place I just left was wanting me.

Chill Space

Sunday afternoon I went to the Garage to work on sketches for my 3-D assignment. Sam was there, too, hat pulled over his headphones and a bag of Dunkin' Donuts on his desk. I bet Sam would reach his freshman fifteen by the end of Wintersession.

I started sketching from *Human Anatomy for Artists*, since I couldn't come up with any ideas for the project.

Plus, maybe the book would say something about the Bowling Ball Phenomenon.

I had left Nate's on Friday feeling bad. Neither of us felt like talking, for some reason. We didn't talk or see each other all of Saturday, either. I decided I wasn't going to call him first. I didn't want to talk to him until he was less distracted. Until his project was under control.

But that's not to say I wasn't checking my answering machine for messages. Every half hour or so that night I'd go outside the Garage to the pay phone. Just in case. And each time, the electronic lady greeted me with the ever dreaded, "Hello, you have no new messages."

Around seven o'clock I guessed he had given up on me. Well, good. He'd been taking up too much of my time anyway.

I went back to the Garage.

Sam was sitting backwards on his stool, arms folded and hanging over the chair back, feet planted on the rungs. His headphones hung around his neck and he was looking at the floor.

"What are you doing?" I asked him.

"I'm in my chill space," he said, still staring ahead.

"Your chill space?"

"Yeah."

"What are you thinking?"

"I'm thinking about chilling."

"What do you mean?"

"Well, Ed wants us to create a space, right?" He turned to look at me. "And my favorite space is my chill space, but, you know, people don't think of it as a space."

"Why not?"

"Because nobody else can go there but me. It's in my head, man."

"I don't buy it," I said. "There must be a way for other people to go there. You're not so different from anyone else. You're just spaced out."

"No way," he said. "When I'm in my chill space it's just me and the thinking machine." He tapped his skull.

"Maybe if you talked more, other people could enter into your thoughts," I said. "If you don't tell people what you're thinking, of course they'll never know what's going on in your head."

He opened his mouth like he was going to say something, but no sound came out.

There was a sudden draft from the door. And arms around my waist.

"Guess what the NECAD film series is playing tonight!" Nate said.

"What."

The Shining!

"Great flick," said Sam.

"Thanks, I know that," Nate said. "That's why I came to get Ellie. We've *got* to go! It starts at eight, so we have to hurry!"

He rubbed his cold cheek on mine. I smelled the frigid air on his jacket.

"How did you know I was here?"

"Well, I just tried calling your place and there was no answer, so I figured this was a safe bet."

Sam was watching us. For the first time I was aware of what it was like to be on the participating side of PDA. In a way, it was uncomfortable having Sam there, but it also made me happy to know that Nate wasn't embarrassed to touch me in public. Maybe he thought of me as his NECAD girlfriend.

"I missed you," he whispered against my face.

"Me too," I whispered back.

It was obvious I wouldn't be getting any more work done that night, so there was no harm in going. Plus, I'd always wanted to see *The Shining*, and here it was playing for free on a big screen.

In the theater's tense darkness, Nate held my hand. Whenever the little boy, Danny, was riding his Big Wheel down the haunted halls, Nate yanked my hand onto his lap and gripped it so tight, he cut off the circulation. He held it hardest at the end, when the Jack Nicholson character was chasing his son through the snowdrift-filled topiary maze.

We ran into Sam on our way out.

"You had enough of the Garage, too?" I asked.

"I couldn't resist *The Shining*," he said, pulling his cap up to make brief eye contact.

There were about two inches of snow on the ground already. It was like the movie hadn't really ended and some maniac might jump out of the bushes at any second.

As soon as we were alone, Nate said, "That guy's got a crush on you."

"Sam?" I asked. "No way. I don't think Sam gets crushes."

"Well, he has one on you. I can tell by the way he was looking at you."

"It doesn't matter," I said. "I'm with you."

Nate tracked snow into my room when we entered my apartment. I got him a towel and asked him to wipe it up. He scowled.

Every time I closed my eyes that night I saw white. Pure white with a man running crazily through it. His face was too far away for me to see who he was. I kept opening my lids to make the image disappear.

"Sorry about your hand," Nate said as I started to doze. "I just about tore it right off during the movie."

"That's all right."

"Having a cute date at a scary film is probably the best thing in the world," he said. "No matter how many times I see that movie, it scares me shitless. I'm glad you were there to protect me."

"Imagine if that was your father," I said.

"I can't," he said. "I never knew him."

"Yeah," I said. "I never did either."

I scooted back so I could feel his skin against me.

That's how we fell asleep. Like two spoons stuck on their sides.

Noise and Heat

The white wind-lashed drifts practically reached the bars on my window. And still it fell in howling whorls.

Classes were canceled. Nate's head shared my pillow.

He was tapping on my stomach with his fingers.

"This is perfect," he said, and kissed my neck.

"Yeah," I said, holding his fingers against my stomach. My rectus abdominus.

The snow was building castles on tree limbs.

"It's strange that winter weather can be the most severe and there's never any thunder or lightning," I said.

He squeezed me tighter.

"Who needs thunder and lightning outside," he answered, "when we've got all the noise and heat we need right here?"

He pulled the covers over our heads.

Worst or Best

"I can't figure out whether you're the worst or the best thing that's ever happened to me," he confessed.

"What do you mean?" I asked. We were sitting side by side on my bed.

We had showered together again, but this time I didn't turn the knob on cold. I hadn't done that since my first shower with Nate.

"Well you know, I like to play around. To try different female flavors. But you — you make me feel like you're all I need. I mean, you're the most sensitive lover I've ever had. I feel this real connection with you, like it's not just sex. You're smarter than the rest. I mean, you don't obsess over your appearance like all the other girls I know. You just seem so much more real."

I picked a pen up off the floor and started fidgeting with the cap.

"Really?" I imagined how I used to look. How I used to spend hours getting my hair and black face paint satisfactorily morose.

"Really. You know, I look around at all these girls and I find myself comparing them to you and they're just not as good. Life's one big competition to them. But you seem to be above all that." He looked out the window, then back at me. "I've never felt this way before."

The pen cap clicked each time I removed it from the tip and replaced it again.

"What about Clarissa?" The words just zipped out of my mouth. I wanted to chase after them and swallow them back up. Instead, I gulped hard on my own saliva.

"Clarissa." He closed his eyes and inhaled deeply. "Clarissa and I have known each other forever. For the last year we've decided to have an open relationship, since we're living in different states. Not that it wasn't open before, but now we don't have to lie about it."

He rolled onto his back and stared at the ceiling.

"I mean, it's hard to sit around and wait for someone," he continued. "Plus, we started fighting a lot once we weren't living near each other. But I still care about her. I guess she'll probably always be part of my life somehow, just because we've known each other so long."

"Where do I fit into this?"

The pen cap popped onto the floor. I picked it up and resumed clicking.

"That's the craziest part about it all," he said, sitting up again. He took a long breath. "I've been dating Clarissa since high school. But I feel like I'm getting closer to you faster, like there's something deeper that's bonding us together."

"What do you think it is?"

"I don't know. I've been trying to figure it out. It's like we came from the same place, like I've known you longer than I actually have."

He put his arm around me and squeezed my shoulder.

"Do you know what I mean?" he asked.

"Yeah. Yeah, I think I do."

I stopped clicking the cap.

"Like when I talk to you about my dad," he said. "Clarissa doesn't comfort me the way you do. She just gives me this look like she doesn't know what to say, and she changes the subject."

"Do you think we're good together because we both never knew our fathers?"

"Yeah, that's a big part of it."

"I feel bad making that connection, though," I said. "You actually never had a dad. I did. I still do. Your situation is a tragedy. My mother just slept around a lot."

"But it amounts to the same thing," he said. "That constant wondering, What if? And wondering, How would I be different if he was there? It's not that your life is worse this way. It's the frustration of never knowing."

"Yeah," I said. "It has nothing to do with the dad I have. I'm sure he's been a better dad than the guy who fathered me, since that guy was probably sleeping around just as much as my mom. He might not have even cared about my mom at all. But I wish I knew that for sure."

He put his other arm around me and pulled me close.

"There are lots of things we'll never know," he said. "But I do know I'm glad I met you."

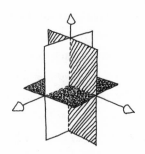

Three Planes

Since classes were canceled on Monday, Ed had to rush through our planes lecture. Not flying planes, but conceptual planes. Planes that define surfaces in space.

There were three types. They moved on three axes. Ralph didn't get it.

"Couldn't there be an infinite number of planes? Things don't just go in three directions," he argued.

"Yes, Ralph, you are quite observant," Ed said. "The planes can lie on any angle. You name it. But they are all variations on one of the three types we have discussed. Can anyone tell me a body part that moves on all three planes? Sam?"

Sam shook his head.

"No, Sam, nice try. It's not the head. And our next contestant . . . Ellie?"

"The arm?" I knew the answer from my anatomy book.

"Correctomondo! The arm! Our grand prize winner is . . . Ellie Yelinsky! Da da-da da da-da . . ." He was singing generic gameshow music and spinning his arms in circles.

Then he swung them side to side. And front to back.

"You can even make them each move on a different plane! Look at them go!" he yelled, watching his arms in awe.

He brought his arms back down.

"Now," he said, "when you begin your three-D projects, I'd like you to think about planes. See if you can build parts that sit on all three planes. You can even incorporate movement!"

He started swinging his arms again.

By the end of class I had decided what my project would be: a giant rib cage. I would pad the inside so you could lie in it. It would be a space for the body to rest, and for the subconscious when you slept. This way I could work from *Human Anatomy for Artists*. And I could use the skeletons in the nature lab for reference.

Plus, Nate's tattoo was always just down the street.

The Final Phase

"No, I know he's an asshole. Everyone knows that!" Sloane said in her little-girl voice. She was with Maura and two other girls, huddled around a library table.

I was at the anatomy shelves, looking for rib cage diagrams.

"So, what are we arguing about then?" Maura asked. Her intonation sounded right this time; it was a real question.

"All I'm saying is he's hot. That's *all*. You can hate someone, but that doesn't change how they look."

I sat on the floor and thumbed through a medical textbook from the shelf, pretending I wasn't listening.

"So would you sleep with him?" one of the other girls asked.

"Well, I don't know," Sloane said, twirling her hair like a shy four-year-old. "I've heard he's a great kisser!"

"From who?" another one asked.

"Oh, I have my sources." Sloane smiled. "But you don't have to look hard to find someone who knows."

I wanted so badly to believe they weren't talking about Nate.

I put the book on the floor and held my fingers up to my ears, trying to make it look like I was just holding my head in my hands in an act of concentration. It didn't matter. Nobody was looking at me anyway.

I looked down at the page my book had been open to the last few minutes. The top of the page had an illustration of the female reproductive system, which I started to copy into my sketchbook. I was about halfway done when the print on the page leapt out at me. The chapter was called "The Final Phase." My eyes drank in the information and I made a list of the darkest-sounding phrases — phrases that would have inspired me to paint back in high school:

> vaginal mucosa
> breasts engorged with blood
> increased secretory activity
> vestibular glands
> psychological stimuli

The rest was all about rising pulse rate and blood pressure, muscular contractions, refractory periods, and multiple orgasms — which women can have, but men can't. Then at the end of the paragraph it said, "While men must ejaculate for fertilization to occur, women do not need to achieve orgasm for conception. Some women, though able to conceive, never experience orgasm."

Of course I knew that guys climax. Duh, you couldn't miss it. But I have no recollection of them ever telling us in sex ed that girls do, too.

I wondered if I had.

I didn't think so. I wondered if other girls I knew did. If other girls who knew Nate was a great kisser ever had.

In the Gutter

We had what Nate called a "quickie."

We'd run into each other by the path to his apartment, and he said he couldn't resist me.

We didn't even take off all our clothes.

"Best painting break I've ever had," he said, zipping his fly. "And now, back to work."

I watched him walk toward the painting studios. He stopped on his way and looked up at an apartment building. He stood there for about a minute before continuing on his way.

As I ran home, something felt different. The cold air didn't fill me with exhilaration. Instead, it seemed to pass through me, as if my body were made of a broken plastic bag, with nothing inside.

Sketching in my bed, I tried to make the empty feeling go away. The old me would've painted a person screaming.

I let my pencil guide my hand.

I wasn't even really sure why I was feeling bad. Maybe Nate and I *aren't* right for each other, I thought. But I quickly drove that idea from my mind. Surely I was overreacting.

I paused to see what I'd been drawing. My marks had started to take the shape of a bowling alley.

I added a ball, rolling down the gutter, completely missing the perfectly placed pins.

Night Guests

Nate's face was there, looking down at me through the window. White-knuckled fists gripping the black bars. Teeth clenched like he was benching Andre the Giant. That's when I realized he was trying to bend the metal.

"You can come in the front," I said. "I'll get the door."

I have to admit, I'd always fantasized about a guy climbing through my window in the middle of the night. But this seemed a bit ridiculous.

By the time I got to my bedroom door, there was this enormous creaking *kaboom*. I turned around. The window was gaping and the curved bars made an opening like a missing tooth. In crawled Nate, tracking snowprints all over my bed.

"What are you doing?" I asked.

He said nothing.

But he came toward me, lifted me and carried me back to my bed and started kissing me all over my face really gently. He laid me down and straddled me, holding me against the mattress by my wrists. Then he raised his head and whistled, as if he was calling a pet.

Before I knew it someone else was negotiating her way through the window.

It was Sloane Boocock. She was trying to hoist herself over the sill, but she kept slipping off. She made little-girl grunts at each attempt, as if she was carrying a heavy load. Nate went to the head of the bed and kneeled on my pillow by the window. Sloane picked up an object I couldn't see. Then Nate put his hands under her armpits to help her. She kicked and wriggled and finally got through, doing a face plant into my mattress. Then she rolled off the bed and onto the floor.

In her arms was a bowling ball.

Nate reached down to help her up to our level, and he told us to sit next to each other on the bed. She handed the big black ball to Nate. He slid his fingers into the holes. Then he took my fingers and pushed them in, too. He started shoving Sloane's in on top of mine.

Nate and Sloane were smiling at each other, as if I wasn't in the room.

I tried to scream, but instead I woke up.

My subconscious obviously hadn't received the news yet; Ellie Yelinsky was no longer dealing with melodramatic symbolism.

That ended in high school.

Skeleton Room

I saw Sam on my way to the nature lab. He was headed up to Main Street.

"Aren't the stores closed by now?" I asked.

"Not Dunkin' Donuts."

"What's up with you and Dunkin' Donuts, anyway?"

"Um, I've sort of got this plan."

"A plan?"

"It's, um, no big deal."

"Come on, you can tell me."

"Well," he said, glancing around nervously, as if to make sure no government officials were eavesdropping. "My goal is to try each doughnut, bagel, and muffin flavor by the end of Wintersession."

"And all this time, I thought you were just a pig!"

He winced, then looked at his shuffling feet.

"I didn't mean that in a bad way," I apologized. "What I meant was, the *real* story is way more interesting."

"Thanks, I think." He cracked a subtle smile.

"Eat a Boston cream doughnut for me," I said. "They're my favorite."

"I like those, too," he said, shifting his cap. "It's one of the first ones I bought."

"Well, I'd better get going," I said, to avoid any awkward silence. "Good luck."

I turned to look behind me when I got to the nature lab at the bottom of the hill. Sam was still standing where I'd left him, watching me. When he saw me look at him, he quickly did an about-face and sped up College Street.

I settled down in the skeleton room at the nature lab. Along one wall was a glass case full of skeletons. There were seven of them, hanging slack-jawed from wires. The monitor took one out for me and hung it on a stand. This was one of the real skeletons. Some of the others were plastic, and had colors showing where muscles would attach to the bones. I could tell this one was a woman; her pelvis was wider than her rib cage.

I wondered what she looked like when she was alive.

I opened *Human Anatomy for Artists* to the rib cage section and started sketching. Ed wanted us to draw diagrams from three vantage points: front, back, and side.

There were so many ribs, I had to keep counting my lines to make sure I had enough.

I wanted this project to look like a mini version of a huge dinosaur rib cage. I'd set it on its back. The spaces between the ribs would be gaps to look through. If you put it outside on a clear warm night, you could peek at the stars.

It would be a good place to lie down and think, to be alone, but to allow nature into your private world at the same time.

I guess *someone* might say I was making a "chill space."

If I Looked Like This

"Why won't you sleep over here anymore?" he demanded one night. "It's like you don't trust me or something."

It was around nine P.M. and I'd gone over to his apartment after working in the Garage for a few hours after class.

"No, I just like sleeping at home. I can't sleep with that racket, anyway." I pointed at the radiator. I was smiling, but I didn't mean to be smiling. My lips were frozen in that position.

I was looking at his paintings of Maura and Sloane. They looked radiant in the pictures, the way you might look after a night with a great kisser.

"What's wrong," he said. "You don't think they actually pose for me, do you?"

"How can I be sure?" I asked. "I've never seen you while you're working. You keep it all so secret."

"You're the only one who knows the plan."

"Right. The *plan*."

He lifted the corner of his futon and pulled out several frayed porno magazines. He shook them at my face. "We're going to the computer lab," he said.

When we got there, Nate dragged two swivel chairs over to a computer. Only a few other people were in the room, quietly clicking on keyboards.

"I'm going to show you what I do," he whispered. "This is everything. But you have to promise not to tell anyone."

"Okay."

"No, 'okay' isn't good enough. Promise."

"Okay, okay, I promise."

"All through high school I tried to be a photo-realist," he said. "I'd go out and shoot pictures of brick buildings, crowded streets, anything with a lot of detail. Then I'd copy the photographs onto canvas with oils. I got really good at it. Some people can't tell the difference between a photograph of the painting and the original photograph."

Then he opened Photoshop files of the Maura and Sloane images I'd grown to know so well. They did look just like the paintings.

"With Photoshop, I don't have to take my own pictures," he said. "All I have to do is create something that *looks* like I took a picture. Here, watch this."

He scanned each of our ID cards into Photoshop. He taught me how to use the tools, how to select facial features and change their size in proportion to the rest of the face. He showed me how to alter the colors.

Nate completely distorted his headshot. He made it look like he'd been running at cartoon speed and landed splat against a glass door.

"Would you fuck me if I looked like this?" he asked.

"I don't think so," I said, laughing.

It was my turn. I used the cloning tool to rub out my eyes, so they looked like patches of skin.

"Would you fuck me if I looked like this?" I asked.

It was fun using that word in this way.

He laughed. "More girls would probably fuck *me* if they looked like that."

He copied his mouth, which was open in the picture because he had been talking when it was taken, and pasted one mouth over each eye.

"How about this," he said. "Would you fuck me if I looked like this?"

"No way."

"What about if I looked like this?" Now, in place of all his facial features was one gigantic mouth.

"Absolutely not."

"Then I guess I'm all right the way I am."

"I guess so."

"What'll it be this week?" he asked himself, flipping through the porn.

He put his hand on my knee and looked at me.

"I want you to know, I discriminate between good porn and bad porn."

"What do you mean?"

"I never use *Penthouse* or *Hustler*," he said. "That stuff is pure porn. The magazines I use have a hint of art in them. Like *Perfect 10*. See, they put their models in natural environments, and natural poses." He laughed. "Okay, maybe not natural, but they're definitely not as degrading as the poses in the hardcore magazines. And here in *Gear*" — he pointed to a picture of a naked woman clinging to a man in business attire — "they get creative. They actually make porn funny."

The next one was *Skin Two*, a fetish magazine. He stopped, satisfied, on a page with a girl dressed in a cat suit. Actually, it wasn't much of a suit; she was wearing ears and a tail attached to garters, and nothing else. On her face were painted whiskers and she was stretching on the ground. Claws extended, ass in the air.

"This is perfect," he said, tapping the cat girl repeatedly. "*Purrrrr*-fect." He gave me one of those *Get it?* grins.

"You know what really *is* perfect?" I said.

"What."

"Sloane looks like she belongs in one of these magazines."

"Yeah, she's got a nice body, doesn't she."

"Her breasts are too big for her head," I said. "It must be easy to transfer her face to the model's body without changing much."

"Yeah, I guess it is."

"Don't you think it's weird that her boobs are so big and she sounds like she's twelve?"

He laughed. "I guess that's why she's so appealing."

Later that night in my bed Nate asked, "What do you think: are Sloane's breasts real?"

It hadn't occurred to me. I'd only known one person who had gotten a boob job, and that was because she was upset that her younger sister had gotten married before her. Apparently, a boob job was the answer.

"I don't know," I said. "Why?"

"People don't just *look* like that," he said. "There's *work* involved in looking like that."

Of Course

The next day, Ed ran into class panting.

"Come on, Dalia, come on!" he called, still out of breath.

He turned to face the door, bent his knees, and smacked the fronts of his thighs.

A golden retriever came bounding in and pounced on him. At her full height, her paws practically reached his shoulders.

"That's my girl!" he said. "That's a good girl!"

We'd been waiting for around fifteen minutes for Ed. It was the first time he'd been late.

"Dalia, meet my students!"

Dalia sat at attention, drooling happily.

"Meet Ellie! Meet Sam! Meet Ralph!"

Dalia barked three times.

"Sorry I'm late, folks!" he said. "I had to get Dalia from the vet this morning! She's been sick and I've been taking her back and forth from home to the doctor, but now she's all better! Right Dalia?"

Another bark.

Dalia responded to Ed so well, it must've been frustrating for her to not be able to speak English.

"How's Dalia feeling?" Ed asked.

She howled.

"Aaoooooooowww!" Ed chimed in with her.

Behind me, Ralph was stifling a laugh. Out of the corner of my eye I saw Sam shooting me a look. I couldn't turn to either one of them for fear of cracking up.

"I hope you don't mind having Dalia here today," Ed said. "If I'd taken the time to bring her home, I would have been even later! And I've already skipped out on you because of her!"

"No, Ed," Ralph said, letting out a laugh. "It'll be cool having a dog around."

"Yeah," I said. "You seem to be having so much fun with her."

"Right on," Sam said.

"Ellie!" Ed shouted. "You've pinned the tail right on the donkey! Dalia's been living with me for seven years, and I've shared my best times with her! Isn't that right, Dalia?"

Dalia panted and let out an enthusiastic bark.

"Show my students how you shake hands," he said. "Ellie, put out your hand for her. Go on!"

I walked up to Dalia and offered her my palm. Sure enough, she placed her paw on top of it.

Then Ralph and Sam had turns.

"Dalia, show my students how you roll over," Ed prompted.

But this time Dalia stayed in place, looking up expectantly.

"Roll over, girl!" Ed shouted.

Still nothing.

"Sometimes she needs some encouragement," he told us.

With that, he got on the floor and rolled on his back.

Then Dalia did the same.

"There you go! That's a good Dalia!" Ed yelled, midroll.

He got up.

"Well, enough playing!" he shouted.

Dalia sat up too.

"Let's get to work! Today we will begin drawing templates for your final projects. I want to discuss materials. Everybody get out your notebooks!"

We took our seats on the stools.

"Are we all ready? Ellie? Sam? Ralph?"

We nodded.

"Dalia, you are exempt from taking notes, but only for today. Is that understood?"

Dalia trotted over to Ed and nuzzled his leg with her head.

Of course not a wife. Of course not a girlfriend. Of course not a boyfriend.

A dog.

Redefining Genetics

Nate was leafing through my photo album. He laughed when he came to a picture of me in pigtails, lying on a giant inflatable ladybug in a pool. The next few pages included various baby shots of me with ladybug garments: a ladybug hat, ladybug sunglasses, a ladybug bib. Lord knows where my mother dug this stuff up.

"Why ladybugs?" Nate asked.

"That's my real name," I said. "Ladybug."

"You have *got* to be kidding me."

"No, that's really it," I said. "Hippie parents."

"Ladybug," he said, grinning. "That's sexy."

"You think so?"

"Absolutely." He kissed me on the lips.

A black-and-white photograph fell out from the back of the

album. It was an autographed picture of Jim Morrison, addressed to my mom. It said:

> Marsha,
> You light MY fire, baby!!!
> Yours always,
> Jim

"Who's Marsha?" Nate asked.

"My mom."

"Did your mom know Jim Morrison?" He was so excited, I felt bad letting him down.

"No," I said. "It's just an autograph."

"Too bad."

"I found this picture in a shoebox under her side of my parents' bed when I was in sixth grade," I told him.

We stared at the picture of the Lizard King for about a minute. Nate began to turn the page, but I held it in place.

And then I added the part of the story I had never revealed to anyone.

"The shoebox was filled with old photos," I said, "mostly of Jim Morrison."

"Wow," he said, "I'd love to have a woman so obsessed with me, she keeps tons of pictures of me hidden under her bed."

"Dream on."

"Come on, you don't think it's possible?" he teased.

"You're no rock star."

"But a sex symbol anyway. I don't need a guitar."

I put him in a headlock and gave him a nuggie.

"Okay, okay," he said with a laugh. "Tell me what was up with the box of Jim Morrison pictures!"

"At the time, I didn't know who Jim Morrison was, so I thought my mother was hiding the box because she had a secret relationship with him."

"Didn't know who he *was*?"

"I was too busy painting and making myself look artsy to think about old-school rock stars."

"That would've been cool though," Nate said. "You know, for your mom to have had a secret relationship with him."

"Well, not really." I was so embarrassed I didn't look at him. "I thought Jim Morrison was my father."

"Just because you found the box?"

"There was more to it than that," I said. "For years I suspected that something wasn't right. Then, once I figured out my parents were only married seven months when I was born, I knew I was onto something. And there were other things — like my mom always telling me to skip over the Father's History section when I was filling out forms at the doctor's office. I used to think, If only I can find some evidence that there was another man, I'll have it all figured out. I thought Jim Morrison was my proof."

"So did you confront your parents?"

"Not yet. I stuck the picture in one of my sketchbooks and didn't take it out for a few years. I mean, I'd look at it every once in a while, but I didn't show it to anyone else. I thought I needed more evidence before I told my parents I knew. My dad's a lawyer. One flimsy photograph wouldn't be enough."

"What *was* enough?"

"Genetics," I said. "Ninth-grade biology. That's what did it. When I learned two blue-eyed parents can't make a brown-eyed girl."

Nate studied Jim Morrison's eyes. "They look dark in this picture," he said.

"Yeah, well anyway, one day after school, I was doing my Punnett squares homework — those genetics charts that show you the odds of offspring inheriting dominant and recessive genes from their parents. I was working at the kitchen table and I had the Jim Morrison picture hidden under my textbook. My mom was in the kitchen, too, working on a project on the floor. I remember this so well. It was such a ridiculous project."

"What was it?"

"She was painting a metal cabinet to look like burned wood."

"Weird. Why?"

"Because the client wanted to be able to stick magnets to it."

"Wealthy people have the most creative ideas!"

"No kidding." I rolled my eyes. "But anyway, I was sitting there with my Punnett squares and I tried to think of a way to ask her why my eyes were brown, without making it too obvious what I was getting at. First I asked if she dyed her hair. She didn't. Then I asked if her contacts were tinted. She said something like, 'I'm *all* natural. Cosmetic technology won't be touching this body.' Whatever it was, she sounded like some commercial for post-hippiedom."

Nate laughed.

"I sat there, tracing my Punnett squares boxes over and over again. Finally I lost it. I started yelling all sorts of crazy things."

"Like what?"

"Oh, I don't know — like, 'Then genetics is a load of crap! If blue-eyed genes are recessive, like Mr. Skripsky says, they can't combine to create brown!'"

"What else?"

"Then I must've said something like, 'Just look at me! My eyes are brown! And they're not even light!'"

"What did she say?"

"Nothing yet," I said. "First I asked her what would happen to science, since I was about to disprove the foundations of genetic theory."

"They'll have to rewrite all biology books because of you!"

"Exactly. I probably said that, too. But she kept on painting. I wondered what Mr. Skripsky would think of her superficial change of a material's properties. I bet he never knew you could turn metal into wood."

"*Another* reason to rewrite science books!"

"It's true," I said. "What am I doing in art school, anyway?"

"Come on, back to the story. Did she ever answer you?"

"Yeah, she finally came over to talk to me. I shoved the picture of Jim Morrison in front of her and asked if this was *him*. She didn't know what I meant, and said 'Him *who*?' And that's when I yelled, 'My father!' She didn't even attempt to stifle her laugh. She said, 'Jim Morrison? Don't you know who that is?'"

"She must've thought you were totally lame."

"Probably," I said. "She explained that he was from the Doors and that her friend had been a roadie for him, and that this friend had given her all sorts of tour photos, including the signed one. I remember her holding the picture up to the light and saying she hadn't seen it in years."

"Yeah, right," Nate said. "She was probably sneaking peeks when your dad was away."

"I doubt it," I said. "But once we'd sorted out who the guy in the picture was, I was almost disappointed. I asked her if this meant Dad's my dad. That's when she stopped smiling. 'Well, he's your dad,' she said, 'but he didn't father you.'"

Nate looked at me expectantly. "And then?"

"And then I flat out asked her who did. 'That I don't know, El,' she said. 'That even *I* do not know.'"

One Thing Left

The next night, Nate was grumpy.

We were sitting across from each other at my table.

Sloane was now getting more compliments than he was. Fritz had called her "fearless," "sensual," "an uninhibited modern woman." He never said anything about the quality of the painting itself.

"That should make you feel good," I said. "He doesn't suspect your stunt."

Nate was tapping his heel like an overanxious drummer. The vibrations traveled through the floorboards to my foot.

"But her work sucks! She can paint her awful kindergarten crap-ola and Fritz won't call her on it. The girl is going to get graded based on *my* skill. I'll bet you anything she gets a better grade than me!"

"Maybe Fritz knows what you're up to. Maybe he thinks you shouldn't use homework as an opportunity to hit on girls."

"But I'm not hitting on her!" he said, slamming his hand on the table. "I'm messing with her mind!"

"Okay, maybe he thinks it's wrong to be messing with her mind in class."

"Well, it's none of his business. Even if I *was* hitting on her, it would be none of his business. That's between me and Sloane."

"What's between you and Sloane?"

"Nothing!" He stood up. "Ellie, don't even try to take this conversation in that direction because there's nothing between me and Sloane, and it's not because there couldn't be, but there just isn't."

"What does *that* mean?"

"It means there's nothing and that's it."

He stared vacantly at the drawing of me and Billy.

"Next week is my last chance. I've got to do something good. Something that'll make her regret she ever went along with this game to begin with."

Then suddenly his face brightened and he jumped to his feet.

"There's only one thing left to do," he said. "And it's risky, but I only have one more shot anyway."

He decided to sleep at home; he had to plan out the next painting.

That night my muscles felt like stretched rubber bands about to snap.

Reflection of Romance

The next night he stayed over.

We were lying under the covers in the dark with our legs entwined.

"I see art as a reflection of romance," he declared after we'd split a bottle of wine.

"How do you mean?" I asked, giggling. Ever since we'd opened the wine, everything he said seemed funny.

"No, I'm serious," he said. "This isn't a joke. I don't usually talk about this stuff with people, but I know you'll get it."

"Okay, so how is art a reflection of romance?" I asked, keeping the corners of my mouth from curling upwards.

"Every mark, every gesture an artist makes is an expression of the lover inside him. We make images we like, we become attached to them, it's hard to see the errors, we fall in love with our creations. We're trying to create the perfect lover."

"I don't think I do that." I imagined myself in bed with Ivan the Terrible.

"It's not something you can control. We all do it."

"What if you're painting morbid scenes? What if you're portraying murder?"

"Love isn't always pretty," he said mournfully. "Sometimes people prefer the rough, untamed side of humanity." He yanked the covers over our heads and wrestled with me in the tangled sheets.

"Well what kind of lover do you think I'm trying to create?" I asked when he finally let me pin him.

"You?" He ran his fingers along the side of my face. "Your work is very careful. Your marks are deliberate. The rhythms in your line quality seem to say something. The subtlety of your modeling somehow affects the viewer — it's hard to tell at this stage, since all I've seen are classroom exercises. But you'll figure it out someday."

"Am I looking to create you?" I asked, giggling again.

"You don't have to look," he said. "I'm right in front of you."

Our laughter melded as he rolled on top of me and kissed my nose.

"Oh," I said. "I guess I just couldn't see you because the lights are out."

The Art Piñata

Sunday afternoon there was a graphic design student-opening at the admissions building. Ryan Brakee was going to do a performance piece. I had never met Ryan, but I'd heard that he was the most daring of all NECAD's performance artists. Once he cultivated maggots in his kitchen, then invited the entire student body over for a dinner party.

At the graphic design show, he'd be presenting the *Art Piñata*. So said the flyers plastered all over campus. I wasn't sure what a performance piece could have to do with graphic design, but I figured the only way to find out was to go.

When I got to the show, people were flocking outside. I decided to stay where the action was and to see the artwork later.

Just before sundown, a circle formed around the courtyard below the balcony of the building, where Ryan stood tying up loose ends. It smelled like someone had died.

People shivered and blew heat into their hands and hollered at Ryan to hurry up. He kept working, never acknowledging the crowd.

When he finally got his act together he raised a huge sack made from an orange tarp. It looked like there was a human body inside. The crowd stepped back, leaving a wide space in the courtyard.

Ryan placed the sack on the railing and shoved it off, so it would land in the center of the ring we'd formed. When the sack hit the ground it exploded with a loud pop.

Candy skidded across the slate.

Limbs went wild, rushing and fumbling for Tootsie Rolls, Milky Ways, and Snickers. After a few minutes someone yelled, "Hey, there's more!" Everybody stopped and looked back up to the balcony.

Ryan hoisted up another sack.

The sun had just about set, so it was hard to see what he was doing. The crowd spread once again, poised and ready to lunge at the next treasure.

We all stood silent and still as if we were in freeze-frame mode.

But this time the sack hit with a deflated thump. Nobody moved except for Ryan, who flew down the stairs cursing. He swooped down on the looming orange lump and tore at the strings. When he got them untied he whipped the flaps open, grabbed a corner of the tarp, and ran away from the crowd. As he dragged the tarp, its contents tumbled out.

A pile of dead raccoons.

But I was struck by the overwhelming odor before I could identify the creatures. People were gagging, coughing, hiding their faces in their shirts like turtles. It was like a cross between curdled milk and how I imagined pickled cow manure would smell. I don't think I'd ever smelled death so distinctly.

People fled.

Most of us hadn't even gone inside to see the exhibit. But it was clear we couldn't stay in the vicinity of the admissions building for the rest of the evening. Or maybe the rest of the week. I'd never heard of an art show where one of the participants purposely sent an audience away.

I clutched my stomach and suppressed the lunge that was sure to make it through my throat at any second.

The All-Curing Remedy

On my way down the hill, Sam caught up with me.

"Hey," he said. "You don't look so good."

"I think I'm gonna puke."

He told me I could take it easy in his room if I wanted. He lived in the freshman dorms right next to us. I took him up on it.

I lay on his bed with my legs raised on some pillows. He sat in the chair at his desk, beside my feet.

"That was pretty rad, huh?" Sam said.

"You liked it?"

"Yeah," he said. "It was like death was let loose out of a bag. And we were supposed to want it like candy. But the smell was so strong we ran away. Like we were too chicken to even go close." He pulled on the brim of his cap.

"I don't know," I said. "I think that guy was just trying to prove something. There was nothing but shock value."

"Yeah, I guess you're right," he said. "You're smart."

"Right now I just feel ill."

I looked at Sam and he looked away. I turned my head to face the cinder block wall at the end of his bed. It was covered with Phish and movie posters. One of them was from *The Shining*, when the Jack Nicholson character is sticking his face through the hacked-up bathroom door. I turned to look at Sam again. Same reaction as before.

"Are you afraid of eye contact?" I asked.

His eyes darted to one side, then the other. Finally he looked me in the eye. "Um, no," he said. "Eye contact is cool."

I laughed and it made me more nauseous. "Do you have anything for upset stomachs?"

"Yeah, I think I do."

He went digging through his sock drawer and came back with a bowl. Not an eating bowl, but a smoking bowl.

"The all-curing remedy," he said, this time sitting on the edge of the bed, next to my legs.

"Will that really help?"

"It'll make you forget," he said. "That's better than helping."

"I don't know," I said. "I'm not really into drugs."

"Don't tell me you've never smoked up."

"I've never wanted to," I said. "Do you think that makes me a wimp or something?"

"No way," Sam said. "I didn't mean to embarrass you. I'm not a good talker." He held the pipe up to his lips. "Do you mind if I take a hit? It'll make me relax."

"Go ahead."

He held the smoke in his lungs for a few seconds before blowing it out through his nose.

I closed my eyes and held my belly.

"I really think this would make you feel better," Sam said. "I'll teach you how, if you want."

"Maybe it's worth a try," I said reluctantly. "Anything to forget that dead raccoon smell."

Sam handed the pipe to me. "You hold it and I'll light it."

I sat up and steadied the stem between my thumb and forefinger. Sam kneeled beside me and struck the lighter over the bowl. The pot glowed like a miniature fireplace.

"Take a drag," Sam ordered.

I inhaled. Then I had a major coughing fit.

"It's okay," Sam said, laughing. "The same thing happened to me my first time." He placed his arm on my back. His arm, hand, and fingers functioned as a single unit. Like a rake.

We passed it back and forth a couple of times, but I took smaller amounts. Then Sam put the bowl on his desk.

"How do you feel?" he asked. His eyes were bloodshot and his words were more drawn out than usual.

I couldn't tell the difference from being sober. And my stomach felt worse. Plus, I was getting a killer headache. "I still feel sick," I said.

"Man, it usually works for me," he said. "Maybe it doesn't work the first time."

"Maybe."

His knee was bouncing fast. "Is your name really Ladybug?"

"It really is."

"Cool," he said. "Wicked cool."

He scooted closer so our legs were touching. The way he moved felt so forced. I stretched my legs out as an excuse to inch away from him.

"Sometimes I try to picture your face," he said. "And I can't. You know how that is?"

"I guess so." He was kind of creeping me out. I had never tried to picture Sam's face when he wasn't around.

He put his paperweight hand on my knee.

"I was thinking about how you said I don't let people into my mind and you're right. I think you understand me better than most people do. Most people just don't understand me."

For the next hour Sam smoked intermittently. I declined his offer for more. As we talked, he kept moving closer and closer to me until I was up against the wall at his bed's headboard.

"You're a really groovy girl," he told me during a long smoky exhale.

"Thanks," I said. "I'm really sort of involved with someone right now."

My head was pounding like I had a heartbeat in my brain.

He coughed. Well, it was a cough or a laugh. "Oh, I didn't mean it that way," he said.

"Sorry," I said. "I was being presumptuous."

He started raving about the raccoons again, but I wasn't paying attention; all I could think was, How do I get out of here without being rude?

It must've been my turn to talk because Sam had gone silent. We didn't look at each other. I sat there, minutes ticking by, fishing for an exit line. I could try something like, Hey, it's been fun smoking your pot and lying on your bed, but I'd rather feel sick in my own room. Or maybe a simple Gotta go! would do.

As it turned out, I didn't need a clever line. Sam was snoring. He had smoked himself to sleep.

I got up to go to the bathroom, which made me dizzy. By the time I made it to the toilet my nausea had returned for a surprise visit. I was glad it hadn't come out on Sam's bed.

I left him there without a note, his arm flopped above the empty imprint on his comforter where I had been.

Sneaking

I couldn't wait to see Nate, after having spent so much awkward time with Sam. But Nate had said he'd be busier than ever with this last painting. He couldn't risk fucking it up.

As I walked home from Sam's dorm, exhausted and empty from puking, I spotted Nate's hair a few blocks down on Artist's

Row. He was standing still, looking up at an apartment building. The same one he'd been staring at before. I thought I'd sneak up on him from behind. Maybe he was done working, and we could hang out.

When I got closer, I saw that he was mesmerized by a window on the top floor. I was doing a good job of being sneaky; he didn't even glance in my direction.

I wanted to know what was in the window, so I stayed on the opposite side of the street from him. I hoped he wouldn't turn around, because I had to stand under a bright street lamp in order to see.

I looked up.

In the window was a silhouette of a busty girl undressing.

I'd gotten there just in time to see her remove her bra and toss it behind her, as if to say, Who cares about this flimsy thing? I couldn't see who she was because the only light came from a room behind her. But those breasts couldn't belong to any other girl at school. They had to be *hers*. Still, I couldn't tell if they were real or fake.

She went to draw her shade. Then she paused and it looked like she blew a kiss out the window. But it was hard to tell from just a silhouette.

I tiptoed to the corner, then sprinted home.

Bonding Moment

Monday in class I avoided looking Sam in the eye. At lunch I directed my attention toward Ralph.

"This is the best assignment Ed's given us," Ralph said. "It's the only thing that has the potential to be worn!"

Sam gave me his standard eye roll, and I pretended not to see.

That evening the three of us were in the studio, working on our projects.

Ralph was making a hollow life-size papier-mâché tree — in honor of me, so he said. He was wearing an apron, and had just started laying the papier-mâché on his wire structure.

"This stuff is so gloopy!" he squealed.

"Better get used to it," I said. "You've got a long way to go."

Sam was making a ladybug out of corrugated cardboard. He was cutting small shapes from a huge cardboard sheet, painting them red, and sticking them together with a glue gun. Like Ralph, he'd started with a wire structure. The degree to which Sam's ladybug blueprints resembled my rib cage blueprints was unsettling. It almost made me want to change my project, but I was too far along to stop now.

I was carving my rib cage out of slabs of blue Styrofoam. First I had glued the Styrofoam pieces together to make a rectangular hut. Then I'd sawed the corners to begin rounding them off. In the end, I wanted to faux-finish it to look like actual bones.

That night I'd been sanding the inside to make the walls smooth. I had to wear a respirator while I was working. Periodically, I would lie down, shut my eyes, and feel the walls for imperfections.

It was like a foam igloo.

Once, while I was checking for lumps, my hand hit something soft. I opened my eyes.

It was Sam's hat.

He was on his hands and knees, leaning into the structure.

"Hey," he said. "This is really cool."

"Thanks." The respirator muffled my voice.

"Can I come in?"

"Yeah, I guess."

He crawled in with a Dunkin' Donuts bag and lay on his back. He pulled a doughnut out of the bag. "I got this for you," he said, handing it to me.

Boston cream.

I removed my respirator and took a bite.

Sam's Adam's apple bobbed as he swallowed hard. "I didn't mean to freak you out yesterday," he said quietly.

"You didn't."

"I did," he insisted. "I don't want things to be weird between us. I just want us to be friends."

"Okay."

"What's going on in there?" Ralph shouted.

"Nothing!" I yelled back with doughnut in my mouth.

"I feel like I'm missing out!" His keys jangled as his footsteps got closer.

He crouched at the opening.

"Hey, it looks like fun in there!" he said. "I'm coming in too! Wait, first I have to rinse this stuff off my hands."

He hurried over to the sink.

"Don't worry," I whispered to Sam. "You didn't ruin anything."

"Make room for me!" Ralph shouted as he pushed my legs in Sam's direction.

I scooted over. Our arms had to overlap for us all to fit. Sam's was stiff, as if rigor mortis had set in.

"Hey, I love that flavor!" Ralph said. "Can I have a bite?"

I held the doughnut in front of his mouth and he bit.

"This project is really something, Ellie," he said as he chewed. "I can't wait to see it finished."

"Yeah," Sam said. "It rocks."

"What a bonding moment," Ralph said.

I couldn't tell if he was being sarcastic, but it didn't matter; for the first time, I was really glad to have him around.

Sacrifice

As I walked home the next night I saw the light on in Nate's room.

I debated whether or not I should go see him. I decided I would. There had to be an explanation for that whole Sloane scene. Something logical. Like his *plan*.

He let me in, then slumped onto the bed.

"I'll be right back," I said, and went to the bathroom.

I sat down on the toilet, and leapt right back up again. There was something hanging from the shower rod.

It was black. It was wet. It was a bra.

A big bra.

I checked the size. D cup.

When I finished up in the bathroom, I walked out with the bra dangling from my fingers by a strap. "What's *this*?" I demanded.

"Oh, that?" He sat straight up. "I forgot that was in there." He laughed nervously. "That's in there because I was using it as reference and I got some paint on it. I washed it this afternoon."

"You *bought* this?"

"Yeah," he said. "It's a nice one, don't you think? I like all the lace."

"I thought you only used photographs."

"Sometimes you need to incorporate still life," he said. "Lace is hard to paint from a picture. I don't know if I'm going to end up using it in the painting, anyway."

"And of course, you wouldn't have borrowed it from Sloane for authenticity, right?" Cool it, I told myself. Maybe he's not lying.

"Ellie, I bought it. End of story."

"Sorry if I'm overreacting," I said. "It just caught me off guard."

"It's okay," he said. "I'm glad you came by. There's something I want to talk about with you."

I sat next to him.

"What's wrong?" I asked.

"I've been thinking."

"Wow, that's amazing."

"No," he said, "I'm serious. I mean, I think things are really good between us, but there's something bothering me. Well, I guess the problem *is* that things are good between us."

"That's a problem?"

"I don't want you to take this the wrong way," he said.

"Take what the wrong way?"

"You're right to feel uncomfortable about me and Sloane."

"I don't feel uncomfortable."

"Yes, you do," he said. "It's okay. It's okay because I do find Sloane very attractive."

"Nate —"

"Don't get upset. Let me finish." He rested his fingers on mine. "Normally, I'd be acting on my instincts. Commitments don't mean much to me, because you never know when you're gonna lose someone. You know what I mean?"

"I think so," I said. But really I didn't.

"And I think I might have a chance with Sloane. I went for a drink with a bunch of people from my class over the weekend. Sloane was flirting like crazy. Rubbing her chest against my back every time she passed me and stuff. As we were leaving, she whispered in my ear that she'd like me to go back to her place."

I held my breath. I was afraid if I let it out I might scream.

"Wait. Don't freak out," he said. "I told her I couldn't go home with her. Do you know why I did that?"

"Tell me."

"You, Ellie. It's because of you. I told her that, too. I told her if she'd asked me a couple of months ago, there would be no question that I'd go."

"What did she say?"

"She said it didn't matter. It made me more desirable, a tougher catch."

"*Great.*"

"Don't be so sarcastic. This isn't a bad thing. I'm just saying I don't want to lose you." He wrapped his arms around my waist.

"What about Clarissa?" I asked, looking at the pictures of her on his wall. "Don't you feel bad about cheating on her with me?"

"Not really," he said. "I think of her as an old friend. She'll be around no matter what happens. We always forgive each other. Besides, she sees other people too. Commitment has never meant much to either one of us in our relationship."

"But doesn't that make your friendship weaker? Doesn't it make you grow apart?"

"I don't think so. Part of the problem with me and Clarissa is that we know each other too well. We know exactly how much we can get away with around each other. There are little things she does that bug the hell out of me, and she knows it. Like she makes a fuss over something small, when really she's mad about something much bigger. She does it just to get attention. I can usually predict exactly how long it'll take her to snap out of it."

"So I don't get it," I said. "Are things good or bad right now?"

"They're good," he said. "They're good. I just wanted to get this off my chest. I wanted you to know about the sacrifice I made."

Tried It

"I tried it," I told him. "I tried it and it didn't work."

"Wait a minute. Back up," he said. "What do you mean, you *tried* it? You mean you smoked it?"

"Yes, I smoked it."

"Lordy, hallelujah, Marsha!" he shouted. "Our daughter's seen the light!"

"I haven't *seen* anything."

"Was it my stuff?"

"No, it was someone else's."

"Wait till you try mine," he said. "I bet it's better."

"I wouldn't know."

"Just make sure you don't do it too much," he warned. "And don't get caught."

"Dad, I think you missed the second part of what I said before. *It didn't work.*"

"Oh, everybody says that the first time," he teased.

"Well, I'll be saying that for my last time too. Because that was it."

"You'll come around."

"Sure I will," I said. "Anyway, I really just called to arrange train times."

Wintersession was ending on Friday, and we had a weeklong break before the real semester started. I was going home to New York.

He picked a time on Friday.

"No, Saturday," I said. "There's a big Valentine's party."

"Okay, but bring the stuff home," Dad said. "Maybe you'll get stoned with your old man!"

"Sure," I said. "And maybe I'll invite all my friends with tie-dyed shirts and VW vans and we'll burn incense while we listen to the Dead."

"Sounds like a party to me!" He laughed, letting my sarcasm roll right over him.

I really had to show more restraint.

Softer Than Clay

The final painting. It was complete. He'd finished it Thursday night and wanted me to see. I went over.

His place was cold. The radiator was broken. He had plugged in a space heater, which made a soft whirring sound.

The painting was actually just a continuation of *Sloanolympia*. But now there was something new. Nate. He was there lying beside her with one hand propping up his head and the other resting on her hip. His fingers drooped over her side, just missing her belly button. She wasn't wearing a lacy black bra.

I stood a few inches in front of the painting. I felt like I was in the same room as them.

"I got the idea from the drawing on your wall," Nate said.

"Right."

"This is probably my best painting yet. And you were my inspiration." He squeezed me tight. "So what do you think?"

"It's really good," I said, trying to sound enthusiastic.

"What's wrong?" he asked, pulling back to look me in the eye.

"Nothing's wrong."

"Why do you keep looking away from me then? You got a problem with eye contact?"

"No," I said. "Eye contact is fine."

"Well, don't tell me nothing's wrong when something's wrong," he said. "I've known enough girls to know what that tone of voice means."

"No, really, it's nothing." It wasn't worth telling him that the painting made me feel weird. I mean, he'd shown me how he made it. And he'd told me he wasn't going to mess around with her. There was nothing to be jealous about. It was a fantasy.

"Fine," he said. "But if you decide to tell me, I'm all ears."

"It's nothing, Nate."

"I wonder what Sloane will do when she sees this one."

"Probably kick you in the balls."

"Maybe," he said, wincing. "Maybe."

That night he bought us a jug of Carlo Rossi. We sat on his futon and drank. I figured I'd have just enough to get pleasantly drunk. But he kept pouring me more and it felt really good buzzing inside me and I kept thinking, In a little while you'll leave.

The room was still cold, except for right in front of the space heater, so I curled up in Nate's flannel comforter. He put my head in his lap and stroked my forehead with his palms. The ceiling spun when I looked at it, and I don't think I could've stood up straight if I'd wanted to.

"You are so beautiful," he told me. "I don't know what I'd do without you."

He got out from under my head and rolled me over to give me a backrub. It was like every ache, every doubt was being kneaded from my body.

He leaned over and whispered in my ear, "I'm sculpting you."

His fingers worked their way under my shirt. Up and down my back. Slowly along my sides. Up and down and up again. Sometimes his thumbs pressed so hard into the back of my neck I could barely stand the pain and sometimes his fingers would glide over my back, leaving goosebumps in their path.

I felt like I was sinking through the bed.

"Your skin is much softer than clay," he said. "Tonight I don't want you to do anything. I just want to sculpt you."

Slip Barrel

In the morning I felt so good I could've dived right into the slip barrel in the sculpture building. It was my last day of Wintersession classes and I was on my way to the final crit. I smooshed my boots into muddy spots along the side of the road. If the puddles were deeper, I would've sunk my entire body into them.

But what I *really* wanted was to be covered in clay. Covered in wet clay with Nate.

Last night, he had touched me until he was too tired. Until he couldn't move anymore. He fell asleep with his arm around me and I fit against him like a missing puzzle piece. There was no sex. Just him groping me until he was too tired to move.

I didn't even feel bad about having slept at his place.

Foundation Finale

Ralph was dressed as a tree. He'd forgotten to leave a hole for his head, so he was constantly calling out to ask if he was about to bump into something.

"No, Ralph, you're fine! Just stay still and you won't run into a thing!" Ed shouted as he snapped away at his tripod. Ed wanted slides of all our semester's work.

Sam's ladybug lay in the center of the room. Even though the sight of it made me squirm in my seat, I have to admit it was well done. A red bulb illuminated the tinfoil-covered interior. And the black dots on the shell gave it a real graphic punch.

"A ladybug!" Ed cried. "Sam, did you know that Ellie's real name is Ladybug? What a coincidence!"

Sam's face turned the color of his project.

Ed liked my rib cage. He asked me to accompany him outside while the other two filled out self-evaluations. We were supposed to tell him how we thought we should be graded and why.

"Ellie," he said, "I don't mean to alarm you, but I want to tell you that you have more talent than most students I see here. And trust me, I've seen hundreds of students. I only say this to one student every three years, it seems. I'm giving you encouragement because I think you should pursue a career in fine art. And if you need help in the years to come, I'd be happy to advise you!"

"Thanks, Ed," I said. "I may take you up on that."

"Ellie, it's not for everyone," he continued. "It's a difficult path to take, but I can tell you have it in you. Don't give up even if it gets tough. It's been wonderful knowing you." Then, as if to compensate for being the slightest bit calm, he started shaking my hand about a mile a minute. "Godspeed!" he shouted.

When we got back in, Ralph, who was still filling out his form, said, "Ed, what do we do if, for example, we think we deserve an A but we think it's too egotistical to say so?"

"You give yourself whatever you think you deserve, Ralph, and I will discuss it with each of you individually when you're finished writing your evaluations. I'm sure everyone will do quite well."

When the evaluations were complete, Ed shouted, "Everybody? Everybody! I have a treat for you all!" He tap danced his way to the center of the room. "For the finale of Gilloggley's Foundation course, I proudly present . . . a slide show of my own work!"

He dashed over to the supply closet and took out a screen.

"Ralph? Ralph! Would you be a gentleman and fetch me the projector?"

Ralph fetched.

"Gather round, gather round!" Ed shouted. "The show's about to begin!"

The three of us laughed as we pulled stools in front of the screen.

Ed flipped off the lights.

I had no idea what Ed's work would look like. I figured it would reflect his spastic nature. Something like Jackson Pollock.

He turned on the projector. The fan began its constant exhale.

The first slide was a charcoal drawing of a seated nude woman with long dark hair, holding her face in her hands. You couldn't see any of her features. Her elbows rested on a countertop and her torso was twisted, so that her rib cage faced the counter and her pelvis faced the viewer.

Everything about her gesture said Sorrow. Or Grief. Or something like that.

The only sound in the room was the projector's fan.

"This is called *Nude at a Counter*," he said. "Original, right?"

Nobody laughed.

The drawing was so elegant. Every muscle was there. The emotion was powerful, but subtle.

"I think everyone's felt like that woman before," Ralph said.

"Yeah," I said. "I have."

"Oh, you don't have to flatter me because I'm your teacher. I'll give you good grades anyway."

"No, it's true," Sam said. "That's rad."

Slide after slide was just as touching as the first one. All of them were sad women. Some were nude, and others were draped in sheets or loose dresses.

"Charcoal is my favorite medium," Ed said. "You can get the best gradations and it gives you more control than paint."

"Do you always use the same model?" Ralph asked.

"Good question, Ralph," Ed said. "Sometimes I hire a model, not always the same one. But for the draped figures I use a mannequin I built. The joints are articulated, so I can move them to the position I want. She's more flexible than a real person, and she sits still longer, that's for sure!"

The last slide was of a woman lying on her stomach in bed, partially draped by a sheet. It was a side view, and one arm hung limply over the edge of the bed. A single finger grazed the floor. That arm said everything about how she felt.

After seeing Ed's slides, I knew why I had come to art school.

A Ladybug for Ladybug

On my way out of the garage, I got stopped by a weight on my shoulder. It was Sam's hand. He asked me if I wanted to get some dinner and hang out. I felt bad about having given him the cold shoulder earlier in the week, so I said I would.

It was Valentine's Day, and I was supposed to meet Nate at a party on Artist's Row later. I had thought I'd take a nap before the party, but the nap seemed less important than not insulting Sam.

"Um, I want to give my final project to you, if you don't mind," he said on our way to the dining hall. "A ladybug for Ladybug."

His eyes bulged, as if he couldn't believe what he'd just said.

"Oh, Sam, thanks," I said. "I don't know if I have anyplace to put it though."

"Well, maybe I could hang on to it for now."

"You should keep your projects," I said. "Someday down the road you'll want to see how much you've improved."

"I don't think I'll ever build anything like this again." He shrugged.

"Well, my mom gave me enough ladybug stuff as a kid to last me a lifetime. I bet you don't have anything ladybugish in your room. You need it more than I do."

"Right." He pulled his cap over his eyes. "If you don't want it, you should've said that to begin with." His steps quickened.

"Wait," I said, rushing to keep up with him. I put my hand on his arm and tugged.

He stopped walking and turned to face me.

"I'm not trying to be mean to you," I said. "I'm sorry if it's coming out that way."

He looked at the ground. "Yeah, it's okay," he said. "It was a dumb idea, anyway."

Preparty

"So, are you, like, dating that guy Nate?" Sam asked when we sat down to dinner.

"Yeah," I said. "I guess you could call it dating."

"You know he's an asshole, right?"

"What do you mean?"

"I've just seen how he is. He's a player. He treats girls like shit."

"Maybe," I said. "But he's different with me."

"Different with you than with all the other girls he fools around with? I swear, that guy would do it with anything that has a vagina." He covered his mouth and gasped. "Sorry," he said. "I shouldn't have said that."

"It's okay," I said. "I've heard that word before. But *anyway,* he's not fooling around with anyone except me right now."

"Is that what he tells you?"

"Yes, and it's true. Let's not talk about Nate anymore, okay?" My face was hot. My heart was pounding.

Sam rolled his eyes. "The nice guys always lose. You've got to be a complete jerk to get a girl. Even a nice girl."

The dining hall air was stiflingly stale.

"I've got to go home and change," I said. "There's this Valentine's party tonight."

"Oh, on Artist's Row?" he asked. "Yeah. I'm going there, too. I can come with you. I mean, I can wait for you to change. Man, I keep saying the stupidest things. I'm trying to make us better friends, but I'm just screwing things up."

"No, Sam. Don't worry so much," I said. "You're doing fine."

"Will you give me another chance to fix things?" he asked. "Maybe if we walk to the party together."

"All right." I didn't want to disappoint him again.

As we started down the snowy hill, Sam asked, "Do you mind going up to Dunkin' Donuts with me? It's still early."

"Okay."

I waited outside while he bought a few doughnuts.

"For the party," he said when he came out. "I get hungry when I smoke."

At my apartment, Sam wiped his feet on my doormat. Then he wiped them again. And again. And again.

"You can come in now," I said.

"I don't want to mess up your floor."

"I think you got all the snow off a few wipes ago."

He stepped inside. The door hit his backpack as it swung shut. "Nice place," he said, wrinkling the Dunkin' Donuts bag with his fingers.

I gathered my dress and makeup and headed for the bathroom.

"Don't do that," Sam said. "I'll go in there. You stay out here."

"That'll be weird, though," I said. "You waiting in the bathroom."

"I can wait outside."

"It's pretty cold."

"Then I'll wait in the bathroom."

"No," I said. "I'm going in there."

"It's outside or in the bathroom," he said. "Your choice."

"Bathroom."

"Just tell me when you're ready." He didn't take off his backpack or coat before entering the bathroom.

I changed into a clingy black dress I'd bought on Main Street a few days earlier especially for this occasion. I thought of telling Sam he could come out now, but I didn't want him to watch me putting on my makeup.

I wore bright red lipstick, the kind you only see on models in makeup ads. I did my eyes up with black eyeliner, but not in the tacky thick way I used to. I hoped I wasn't overdressed. But hey, it was a Valentine's party; I had to dress a little risqué.

"Okay, I'm ready!" I called.

The door opened slowly. Coat still zipped, backpack still gripping his shoulders.

He blinked hard, then opened his eyes wide.

"What?" I asked.

"I know you don't want to hear this," he said, "but I don't think I've ever seen anyone look so beautiful."

"Thanks, Sam."

It's strange; that was the most direct thing he'd ever said to me, but it felt the least awkward. Flattering, even. I wanted to go back and hear him say it again.

We made eye contact for a few seconds and this time I looked away first.

No, I told myself. You can't think of Sam that way.

Hearts in the Basement

Almost everyone in the basement was dressed in red. Hearts dangled from strings taped to the ceiling. Ella Fitzgerald was singing "Lover, please be tender . . ."

In a dark corner, a group of topless girls with red hearts painted on their nipples waited for a camera to flash. They were trying to coax a flat-chested friend into joining them. But she was either not as daring or not as drunk as they were, because she maintained her position against the wall, fully clothed, arms folded across her chest.

I was so amused by this scene that I almost didn't realize the photographer at whom the well-endowed girls were puckering their lips was none other than Nate Finerman. Two of the girls, I realized, were Maura and Sloane.

One girl busted her way out of the group and grabbed the camera from Nate's hands, pushing him into her former position. The girls immediately pounced on him, fighting over who got to be closest to the male of honor. Sloane wriggled her way to the center for one of the photos and stuck her vinyl miniskirt-clad leg across Nate's waist.

At some point during the photo session Nate noticed that I was watching and he winked at me. He tried to walk toward me, but the girls yanked him back. When he attempted an escape, they tackled him to the floor. He poked his face out from among the girl pile and gave me a *What can I do?* face.

I almost left the party at that moment, but when I turned around I ran into Ralph. He had a question he'd been *dying* to ask me.

"Ellie, I've just *got* to know. Have you considered *wearing* your three-D project?"

"No."

"Well, maybe sometime next semester we can collaborate on an outfit. I *love* the idea of wearing your insides on the outside."

Nate had finally escaped from the mountain of girls. He ran up to me and pulled me around so I wasn't facing Ralph anymore.

"Hey, sexy," he said.

"I want to go," I whispered.

"Why?" he asked. "You just got here!"

"Nate, I just have to go."

"Oh, come on, wait for me," he said. "I want us to leave together. It *is* Valentine's Day and all. Plus, it's the last night before you leave. Let's hang out just a little longer."

"Well, okay," I said. "But not *too* long."

"I've been thinking all day about being with you tonight. We'll mingle a while and then meet up." He kissed my forehead.

Ralph was gone by the time I turned back around.

I wandered the basement, looking for familiar faces. It was

painfully evident that I didn't know many people. And this was a pretty small school.

I found Sam sitting alone in a corner, smoking a joint.

"Hey, Ellie," he said with squinty bloodshot eyes.

"Hey, Sam." I sat down next to him.

"You want a hit?"

"No, thanks." I did, however, share his last doughnut. Boston cream.

"Saved it for you," he said.

I hoped my face wasn't as red as it felt.

He balled up the Dunkin' Donuts bag and stuffed it in his backpack.

"What do you keep in there?" I asked. "That thing looks like it weighs you down."

"Just stuff. I like to be prepared."

He put out his joint and slid it behind his ear. Then he rooted through his bag and pulled out his Diskman and headphones.

"There's this," he said. "And these." A handful of batteries. "The Diskman eats them up. And I keep this around in case I run out of batteries." He yanked an adapter out by its wire. "None of it would be any good without these." There must've been at least a dozen CDs. All Phish and Grateful Dead, as far as I could tell.

Then, of course, he had his rolling papers, tobacco, and lighter.

Next was his monster-size hardcovered sketchbook. He showed me a page with a tallied list. There were three categories: doughnuts, muffins, and bagels. Each flavor had a single mark beside it. Except one. Boston cream had three.

"You finished?" I asked.

"Tonight," he said, beaming.

"That's a lot of stuff to carry around all the time."

"It gets heavy sometimes," he said. "But it's comforting to keep the things I need with me wherever I go."

Nate found me. Said he wanted to leave. Held his hand out to help me up.

"We'll finish this conversation later," I told Sam clearly, so Nate would hear.

"Right on," Sam said after lighting up again. He waved good-bye with his joint.

Nate and I walked slowly up the rickety basement stairs and didn't say anything until we got outside.

"There's cream on your chin," he said without looking at me.

I wiped it off and licked it from my fingers.

"There's a nipple mark on the corner of your mouth," I said.

It was smudgy, like the kiss marks you get from your grandma.

He wiped at the wrong side.

"No, *there*." I pointed closely at the mark, but didn't touch it.

He never wiped it off completely.

"So have you been hanging out much with that guy?" Nate asked.

"I guess," I said. "Sam and Ralph were the only other people in my Foundation class, and Ralph is a little hard to handle at times."

"That Sam guy probably thinks he can get girls by being all quiet and mysterious, but it's all an act. You know that, right?"

"Maybe," I said. "Why don't you like Sam? You don't even know him."

Our shoes crunched on the snow. Like it was a snack.

"You know, I just have a hard time seeing people with fast food," he said. "This is so embarrassing to admit because I know it sounds crazy. But it's especially hard seeing them with you."

"Sam didn't have fast food."

"Dunkin' Donuts!" he cried. "They may not serve burgers, but they're just as much fast food as Burger King. They have a drive-thru, for crying out loud!"

"You watched us eating doughnuts?"

"I just happened to see. Why, were you trying to hide it?"

"Of course not!"

Nate packed a snowball with his bare hands.

"This doesn't make any sense," I said. "You know I have more sympathy for your problem with fast food than anyone, and I'll always feel weird walking into a McDonald's because of your dad. But if I want a doughnut, I'm gonna eat a doughnut!"

"I just thought we had an understanding," he said, still packing his snowball.

"Are you jealous?"

"Are you kidding?"

"No," I said. "I feel like you're looking for excuses to be mad about me hanging out with another guy, which is so stupid."

"I'm not saying I'm jealous," he said, passing his snowball from one red hand to another, "but even if I was, why would that be *stupid*?"

"Because *I'm* making myself *not* be jealous."

"Why?"

"So we can stay together."

"Who are you jealous of? Clarissa?"

"Sometimes it's Clarissa!" I shouted. "But right now it's Sloane! I thought you were staying away from her!"

"I was!" he yelled. "I am!"

Then he threw the snowball with all his might, screaming "Aaaagh!" It hit the side of a house across the street and exploded into white powder.

I was fighting back the tears.

"Ellie, can't you see that since we've been together I've been trying harder than I've ever tried to be honest? Ever since I met you, I've been trying not to mess around. And I know it would really hurt you if I did because messing around is the whole reason you don't know who your dad is. But sometimes a guy's just gotta have some fun. It doesn't mean anything to me, and it's not so bad anyway. But I've been trying my hardest! For you! And it hasn't been easy!"

"What do you mean by *trying?*" I asked, concentrating on not crying.

A car passed us, headlights illuminating our stillness.

"Do you really want to know?"

"No," I said quietly. "Not really."

"Well, I guess this is a Valentine's evening down the drain."

I nodded. I was afraid if I opened my mouth, tears would start spouting.

"Let me walk you home," he said.

We walked slowly beside each other without talking. When we got to my door, he asked if I wanted him to come in. I shook my head no.

"I'll see you when you get back then," he sighed. "You'll be back Friday?"

I nodded.

"Have a good trip." He sounded defeated. "Call when you get in. All right? Make sure you call."

He took my hand in his and brought it to his lips for a kiss. His hands were still cold and a little wet from the snowball. His lips were warm.

"Okay, bye," was all I could say.

Going Home

In the morning I caught a train to Manhattan.

Towns whizzed by the windows as the train whistle blew.

I was trying to draw my view from the window in my sketch-book. I wanted to capture the movement, like in Ed's fish assignment. I thought that concentrating on such a difficult task would keep my mind off Nate.

It didn't.

I kept losing interest in the window blur and thinking about Nate's body. I sketched his back, with the rib cage tattoo. I wondered what it would look like if his entire body was tattooed with the underlying bones. I tried drawing a few parts like that, but it was hard to do from memory. Arms and legs were so complicated.

Maybe I should've made up with him last night, I thought. After all, he *had* said he was really trying to change for me. If he thought I didn't appreciate that, maybe he'd stop trying.

I drew the back of Nate's leg. I made his gastrocnemius flexed, the way it looked when he stood on his toes.

I thought about how I'd yelled at him. I should've been more calm and tried to work things out. I had let my emotions get the better of me.

Maybe I should've just stayed at the party and kept talking to Sam.

I looked out the window and tried to draw the passing trees. But what I ended up drawing looked like Nate's hair. I pressed harder with my pencil, to block out the Nateness and make the image more treelike.

The heavy lines only made my drawing look more like thick tufts of hair than like thin branches. I tried erasing certain parts but that didn't work either. Then I erased the whole thing. That just left me with a lighter version of the original drawing. I didn't want to look at it anymore.

I drew a big X over the page, then scribbled and scribbled, covering up the hair.

But I had to stop before concealing all my old marks; the pencil's tip broke and the remaining wood shards ripped through the paper.

Absolutely Bananas

"It's a great way to lower your sex drive," Dad said, patting me on the back. "You teenagers have such raging hormones, they need all the help they can get."

"Oh, give it a rest," Mom sighed. "Don't turn her into a stoner, all right?"

We were sitting in the kitchen, waiting for our pizza delivery.

My dad got up and paced around the table.

"I don't think you get it," I said. "I tried it once and I didn't even like it."

"Which is absolutely fine," Mom said, glaring at my dad.

Dad paced his way out of the room.

Mom leaned in close and touched my arm. "So, I'm dying to know — are you seeing anyone?"

The doorbell buzzed.

"I'll be right down!" Dad shouted into the intercom in the hallway.

"I've been dating a guy," I said.

"That's great!" she said. But her face looked relieved, like what she really wanted to say was, "Finally."

"It's all right."

"Just make sure you use protection," she cautioned. "You never know where people have been."

And sometimes you do, I thought.

Dad came back with the pizza.

"Sorry to dwell on this raging hormones thing," he said, "but I can't imagine growing up as a kid in the nineties. You have to worry about birth control *and* AIDS. It would drive me absolutely bananas."

Lying Awake

I thought about Nate that night. I wanted to think about feeling him in bed, about his soft thick hair against my skin. But every time I tried, I pictured that snowball smashing against the building.

I wanted to make myself forget the images of him at the party and of our fight.

They wouldn't melt.

Exciting Isn't Everything

"Were the sixties a total blast?" I asked my mom.

We were chopping vegetables for dinner that night.

"A total blast?" she asked. "That doesn't sound like something *you'd* say."

"It's something my friend at school said. I think he wishes he could've been alive then."

Mom chopped two carrots for every one I got through.

Grandma and Phil were coming over.

"You know, those days were exciting," Mom said, slicing a pepper. "But exciting isn't everything."

The Other Relatives

"Looks from the mother, brains from the father," Grandma said when my mother told her I'd gotten an A in Foundation class. My report card had come that day.

"Mom!" my mother yelled in defense.

"Marsha, you know you never did well in school." Grandma always had a way of shutting her up. She turned to me and raised one eyebrow.

We were all sitting at the table. Mom and Dad at each head, Grandma and Phil across from me. Beside me was an empty chair.

The chicken was in the oven.

On the table was Mom's traditional assortment of vegetables and dips. I think this premeal snacking was Phil's favorite part of family gatherings; I've never seen anyone else eat chopped liver with such gusto. Mom had placed a dish full of it by Phil's plate.

Grandma and Phil weren't really married, but he was my Grandpa's identical twin and he agreed to take care of Grandma after Grandpa died. Now Phil shared her bank account and her bed.

"Ladybird," Grandma said.

"Bug, Mom. Not bird," my mother scolded.

"To you she may be a bug, but to me she is a bird." She never missed an opportunity to mock my mother's hippie days. "Lady, have you heard about the call? The one from the PBS?"

"We thought we'd let you tell her," Dad said.

"Okay, well I'll do it then," Grandma said.

Phil spread some chopped liver on a celery stick.

"A few days ago I got a call from the PBS. They want me to do a talk on the television. About the Holocaust."

Grandma was a Holocaust survivor. She rarely talked about it with us. As far as she knew, she was the only surviving member of her family.

"Are you gonna do it?" I asked.

"Well, I don't know."

"I told you, you shouldn't," Mom said. "It upsets you too much."

"But it would be a great educational tool for generations to come," Dad said.

"They'll find other people," Mom said.

"Not if everyone has this attitude," Dad said.

The oven timer rang. Mom got up to get the chicken.

Phil dipped a carrot in his chopped liver dish. It was almost empty.

"Save some for dinner," Grandma warned him.

"Of course," he nodded. "What would I do without this woman?" It was the first time he'd spoken since we sat down.

"I don't know what you should do about PBS," I said.

"Right. This is what we were speaking about," Grandma said.

"I just can't imagine going through something as awful as the Holocaust. I mean, it sounds like this is a good cause. But who am I to say whether it would be good for you or not?"

Mom came back with the chicken and started serving Phil.

"People, they go through the tough times and they make it okay," Grandma said. "My husband passed on, but I'm all right."

Of course you are, I thought. His replica is right beside you.

But how did she ever get through losing her entire family? I wondered what the other relatives I'd never met were like.

Phil cut a piece of chicken and spread chopped liver on it. He raised it in the air and said, "Without this woman, I would've forgotten to save the chopped liver for the meal. She's always looking out for me!"

Grandma smiled at him.

My parents shot each other looks, as if to say, What happened to Grandpa?

He never liked chopped liver.

A Murderer's Advice

Ivan was there. In New York City. That's what the lady at the Met said on the phone.

I wished I knew how to drive the subway, so I could make it go faster.

At the Met, I passed the rest of the nineteenth-century Russian paintings. They and the cooing crowds were blurs in my peripheral vision. Finally, I got to the room of Repins.

There he was. Larger than life. Grasping his bleeding son on Oriental rugs. I sat on a bench in front of him.

Ivan was the only one who would understand what I was going through.

"I shouldn't have done it," I wanted to say to him.

"Tell me about it," he would've said, but in Russian.

"Look at us. Two losers," I'd say. "Your son, my virginity — gone forever."

But that's where my fantasy ended.

What could Ivan say to that? "Oh, honey, you've got a lot to learn" or, "Come back when you've killed someone. Then we'll talk."

Through the Wall

"She doesn't have that sad look anymore, but she still looks sad," Dad said.

I heard him through the wall, talking to my mom, as I tried to fall asleep.

"She'll be fine," Mom said. "She's adjusting to her new life."

"I think she's still not fitting in."

"Well, I don't think the pot is gonna do it."

"Can you imagine how cool we would've thought our parents were if they'd given us pot?"

"We might have thought they were a little strange."

"I just wish we could communicate. You know, real father-daughter bonding. But she always gets so sarcastic on me."

"You don't seem to mind."

"I laugh it off so she doesn't think it bothers me. And so we don't get in a fight."

"Maybe that's part of the problem."

"No, the problem is that she's not mine," he said. "That's always been the problem."

I'd never heard him admit I wasn't his child before. I pressed my ear against the wall.

"Oh come on," Mom said. "That's never bothered you."

"Marsha, it bothers me every day. Every day. Every time I look at her, trying to imagine whose features she has." His voice got closer, then went farther away again. He must have been pacing. "But I never say anything about it because I know I can't change it."

"She might as well be yours. You raised her."

"I know," he said. "But I wish she was *really* mine."

"That's a fine wish," she said, "but I don't think that would change the communication problems you're having."

"I do. I think she wouldn't be so hostile toward me. She knows, whatever I say, I'm just a stand-in."

"I think if you try getting closer to her with something other than narcotics, she might respond more favorably."

"Like what?"

"I don't know," she said. "This is something you'll have to come up with on your own." The bed squeaked. She must've sat up. "Or else it won't be genuine. Maybe you should stop thinking about what *you* liked doing as a kid, and think about what *she* likes to do."

"You're right," he sighed. "As usual."

His footsteps came up to the wall between us, then stopped.

"I don't know why you're getting so worked up, anyway," she said. "We never would've been able to have her on our own. Not with your condition."

This was the first I'd heard of a "condition." I'd always assumed they didn't have more kids because the others would've been more purebred than me and I'd feel bad.

"I know, I know." His pacing picked up again, faster this time.

"And if it wasn't for Ellie showing up the way she did, we may never have gotten married. She's the one who brought us together."

"Marsha, everything you're saying makes so much sense. And I've run it all through my head millions of times. That's why I've never said anything about it. But still . . ." He paced close to the wall. "I just . . . I just wish it were different."

A Closer Look

My dad took the next day off, since I was leaving New York that night. I asked him to go to the Met with me in the morning.

He raised his eyebrows. "What, has someone discovered a new way to paint naked ladies?"

"Seriously," I said. "There's something I want you to see."

It was early, so there weren't many people at the museum yet.

"Aren't we going to look at the rest of the show?" he asked as I marched straight for my favorite room.

"Later."

We sat on the bench before Ivan.

"Reminds me of your old work," he said.

"It's way better than my old work."

For a long time, we didn't talk. The room was empty, except for us and a guard.

I don't know what my dad was thinking, but he didn't stop looking at the painting. He didn't get antsy either, like he usually does at museums.

When he finally did get up from his seat, it wasn't to make a beeline for the exit, but to take a closer look at Ivan's eyes.

Wild Trip

"Where's your beret?" Mom asked when we came home.

"What beret?" Dad said.

"You two were gone so long, I thought maybe Ellie had turned you into a fanatical art lover."

"Well," he said, "we spent most of our time looking at Ellie's favorite painting. Then we saw the rest of the show and waited in a long line to buy this book."

He took the Repin book out of my hands.

"I wanted to get Ellie a souvenir," he said as he sat down at the table. He opened the book and flipped through the pages.

"You sure you didn't get the book for yourself?" She winked at me.

"No. It's a present for Ellie," he said without looking up. "I'm just trying to find that painting she likes. You've got to see this guy's eyes. They're bugging out like he's on some wild trip or something."

He finally found the right page and showed my mom.

"That's a nice one," she said. "Hey, El, you want to help me get some food for your last home-cooked dinner?"

"Sure."

When we returned from the store, Dad was still looking at the book.

I decided to stay home the rest of the weekend.

Messages

When I got back to school I opened my backpack and found a box of condoms in the front pocket with my pencils and toothbrush. Thanks, Mom.

There were six messages on my machine. One from my mother, calling to make sure my trip was all right, and the rest from Nate. They went like this:

> It's Nate.
> Give a call when you get in.
>
> Hey, where are you? Thought you'd be back by now.

So, uh, you were supposed to call when you got back, right? Call me.

Come on, it's not that bad, Ellie. I want to make up with you. Don't be so stubborn.

All right, this is the last message I'm leaving. If I don't hear from you by the end of the day, I'm assuming we're not friends.

I was two days later than I planned. Big deal.

I automatically picked up the phone to call him back; that's what you do when someone leaves you a message. It's what I said I'd do on the machine.

But I hung up after dialing the first three numbers.

My hands were clammy and my armpits were sweating.

I sat by the phone for about ten minutes, putting my hand on the receiver and then removing it again.

The phone rang.

I let it ring four times and just as the machine began to chime in, I picked it up.

"Ellie. I missed you," he said. "I need to see you."

An ambulance whined on his end of the line.

"I thought that was the last time you were calling."

"I lied."

The ambulance crescendoed as it passed my window.

Snow was settling over the streets.

"Can I come over?" he asked.

"Well . . . okay."

Missed

He held me and kissed my entire face. Told me he'd never missed anyone this much before. He was surprised by how often he thought about me. How clearly he could imagine the smell of my shampoo. How many times he held conversations with me in his head.

Melted snowflakes dripped off his jacket.

"Clarissa's been here since Thursday and all I can think about is you," he said.

"When did she leave?" I asked tentatively.

"Well, she's still here. I told her I had to go see you because you just got back."

"And she was cool with that?"

"Pretty much," he said. "She knows we can't spend all our time together. It would be too intense."

"And does she know . . . what things are like between us?"

"Sure, we tell each other about everyone we date. I mean, it's hard to go so long without getting some. She knows that. Even a month is pushing it. What she doesn't know is how hard I've fallen for you."

"Oh."

"I want you to get to know her," he said. "It'll make me feel better."

"I don't think that's a good idea," I said. "For anyone."

"It's up to you," he said. "I just think if the two of you got along, this would be much easier. We'd all have some sort of understanding."

"I'm not sure that's an understanding I'd like to have."

"Fine," he said. "But if you change your mind, the offer still stands."

He hugged me briefly before he left.

About an hour later, I called him.

"I'm coming over," I said, pulling my boots on.

It was still snowing lightly.

"Great," he said. "We'll be here."

I decided I wanted to find out about this girl. This girl who would let him get away with anything.

What's Up with the Fire Hydrants

She was painting her nails iridescent pink as Nate and I flipped through his sketchbook. The three of us were sitting on his futon. We came to a page with a fire hydrant morphing into a woman crying.

"What's that?" I asked.

"I did that from an idea I had about Clarissa."

She put the nail polish on the floor. "That's me?" she asked, inching closer.

"Well," he said, "I saw a fire hydrant going off one day and when I got home I realized how much it reminded me of you when you cry."

"Oh." She pursed her lips, then resumed painting.

The radiator banged.

Nate got up to go to the bathroom. After his footsteps ceased and the door clinked shut, Clarissa said, "I wondered what was up with the fire hydrants." She wrinkled her brow and looked at a papier-mâché model of a life-size fire hydrant, the one that had been in the fountains show. "Did you know what those were about before?"

"No," I said. "You've heard as much as I have."

With all the fuss about the Sloane Collection, I'd almost forgotten about the fire hydrants.

The toilet flushed and Nate came back.

"Damn!" Clarissa shouted at her nails. "I fucked up again!"

"It's no big deal, cutie," Nate said, rubbing his hand over the shaved side of her head.

"You just don't understand," she said. "Ellie understands, don't you Ellie?"

"I haven't painted my nails in a long time," I said, shrugging.

The radiator banged over and over in the same pattern as it hissed steam.

"Well, you probably remember that it looks stupid when nail polish gets on your skin," she said.

"It never bothered me much."

Nate sat between us and put his arm around her. "You don't have to get worked up about something so trivial," he said.

She shook his arm off and whined, "It's not trivial!" Then she ran to the bathroom and kicked the banging radiator before slamming the door.

"Oh, man, not again," Nate said as he ran after her. He tried the knob, but to no avail. "Come on, Clarissa. Don't be an idiot."

No answer.

He walked back toward me. "I give her twelve minutes," he said, looking at his watch, like this was some private joke between the two of us. "How about you?"

"I have no idea."

I stood by the window. It was snowing harder than before. A couple of inches had already accumulated.

He massaged my neck.

"You never overreact like that," he said.

"Maybe sometimes I should."

We watched the snow fall. His hand crept up to my head.

"What are you thinking?" he asked.

"I should go," I said, lifting his hand from my scalp. "I'm obviously not spending the night or anything."

"That might be fun." He grinned.

I had this urge to gouge my elbow into his ribs.

"No," I said sternly. "It wouldn't."

When the bathroom door cracked open, Nate checked his watch. "Twelve minutes!" he announced, and greeted Clarissa with a nuzzling embrace.

He had his back to me as he hugged her. I grabbed my jacket and snuck to the door without a sound. Clarissa's eyes followed me, looking satisfied.

I didn't say good-bye or wait to see if he turned to watch me leave. I only left the door wide open, letting the drafty air take my place.

Tailored Tracks

With a running start, I could slide about ten feet in the slippery snow. The sky had just reached its peak of darkness and the final flakes fell while the stars flickered.

After sliding a few times, I walked, compressing the snow under my soles. It squeaked like clean hair, but louder. The flakes were so big you could almost see the snowflake shape.

I made sure to place each step I took in a spot untouched by another shoe. That way my footprints would be as defined as possible.

I had a feeling it was the last time I'd be taking that path.

Should Have

Sitting in my bed that night, I stared off into space. My room was cold, and I wished I could've had some extra body heat.

Maybe when Clarissa's gone, I thought.

No, I told myself, she'll be back. And if not her, then someone else.

I picked my sketchbook up from the floor and drew everything I remembered about Nate. I even drew his paintings. When I was done drawing, it was clear: We weren't right for each other. Too many of my drawings were about the other girls in his life.

I should have elbowed him in the ribs.

Rage Against Human Dictionaries

"That's it, that's it, clear 'em all out of here," Gregg directed. "We won't be needing those." He sat on a drawing table in front of the chalkboard. His lanky legs dangled and he was gripping the front of the desk.

A bunch of hair-dyed, tattooed, pierced students were pushing the rest of the drawing tables against the wall. The legs screeched as they dragged across the linoleum floor.

It was my first day of real NECAD classes; Foundation Two. Gregg Cramroy was supposed to be teaching us advanced drawing, 2-D design, and 3-D design. We met in a classroom in the design building.

Gregg's jet-black hair was combed and gelled into perfect one-inch spikes and his rectangular metal glasses gleamed under the fluorescent lights.

I helped a girl with fishnet stockings push one of the last tables aside.

When the center of the room was finally empty, Sam walked in. He was the only person in the class I knew. He was also the only one aside from me with natural hair color and no body art. How did these people find time to keep up such appearances with all the work we were expected to do?

"Hey, Sam," I said. "How was your week off?"

"Really good," he said, pulling his cap up, rather than down. With the cap covering his eyes most of the time, I'd never noticed that there were brown bursts in the center of his blue irises.

Gregg clapped his hands twice and shouted, "Okay, everyone, grab a chair! We'll be putting them against the wall, too, soon, but you might as well be comfortable for now."

We all pulled chairs into the clearing in the center of the room.

"I'm Gregg," he said, "for those of you I haven't met."

His legs were swinging while he spoke.

"Now, we need to straighten out a little misunderstanding before we start. This catalog" — he waved the NECAD course catalog in the air — "this catalog says I'll be teaching you the second semester of drawing, two-D, and three-D. Well, it looks like that won't be happening."

He slowly shredded the booklet with his hands.

A guy with a blue mohawk whooped.

A girl in a pink babydoll dress and a barbell through her nose shouted, "Wicked!"

"But we *will* work in here," Gregg continued. "Oh, we will work. But we'll be making *real* art!"

More whooping. Even Sam let out a "Right on!"

I didn't say a thing.

"Let me tell you a bit about myself before we begin," Gregg said. "Ten years ago I went to a small art school in the Midwest. That school tried to drag me down, tried to kill my artistic impulses just like this school is trying to do. They had us drawing from casts of classical sculptures, they tried to teach us anatomy, to make us memorize all the terms for the muscles and bones. And you know what I said?"

His legs were swinging harder.

"I said to hell with it! I said I came here to express myself, not to become a human dictionary! And so I took one of those plaster casts and I threw it out the window and watched it smash into pieces on the pavement. Then a bunch of my buddies came and tossed some others out the window, and by the end of the night they were all gone. All gone. We were kicked out of school, and that was the beginning of my art career. I'm new here at NECAD, and I've come to free all of you, to make sure that none of you fall into the trap of becoming human dictionaries!"

Everyone except me was clapping and cheering and whistling, like they were at a rock concert.

"Thanks, thanks," Gregg said. "Now, I want to get started ASAP. Let's not even bother with attendance. I don't really care if you're here or not. It's your loss if you skip. Anyway, names aren't important. It's what you do that matters."

He jumped down off his desk.

"Everyone push your chairs against the walls and come back to the clearing and lie on your backs," he instructed.

I walked slowly and waited until almost everyone was on their back before I joined them, just in case this was a joke.

The floor was cold and hard.

If I had to be lying down right now, I'd rather be in my bed.

When everyone was in place, Gregg said, "Now, I'm going to give you a series of instructions. Some of them may sound a little strange, but bear with me. I want you to totally lose control. Forget about what's normal and what's weird." He made quotation marks with his fingers around *normal* and *weird.* "You are about to feel what it really means to be an artist."

He clasped his hands together and took a deep breath.

"First of all, you need to spread out. Give yourself enough room to make a snow angel, and then some."

I stood up and walked to the back of the room, stepping over the people in my path, and lay down. Sam and a couple of others did the same.

"Good," Gregg said. "Now I need you to close your eyes. And keep them closed. Really. No cheating."

It sounded like a kid's game of hide-and-go-seek.

"Now imagine that you're lying on hot sand."

That wasn't easy on this floor.

"The sun is beating down on you and you're drifting off to sleep. You don't even realize that the water has been creeping up to your toes. Feel the waves tickling your feet. They crash at your ankles, but you're not bothered because you're so relaxed. Breathe in through your nose and out through your mouth."

Everyone in the room was breathing in synch.

"That's it," Gregg said. "By now the water has reached your knees and is making its way to your thighs."

I wanted to open my eyes. Just to make sure everyone else was still doing this.

"Now it's crept up to your bellybutton. The lower half of your body is floating."

Is that possible? Can half of you float while the other half is on the beach?

"You are more relaxed than you could ever imagine," Gregg informed us. "The waves have gotten to your shoulders, and now to your head, and now they're lifting you away from the beach and you're floating. Breathe in and out. In and out."

I heard the breathing. But still, this could be a trick. They could all be sitting in place, laughing silently at me, the fool who fell for it.

"You're floating, but you find that you can move around in the water without fear of sinking, so you rock back and forth. Left to right. You rock just to the point where you could roll over, but you don't pass that point. Back and forth. Back and forth. Now very slowly I want you to roll onto your stomach, but do it carefully so you don't hit the person next to you. And keep your eyes closed. Over to the left. And back over to the right. That's it."

I folded my arms across my chest when I rolled on my stomach, and I lifted my head so I wouldn't get dirt on my face. I hoped I wasn't getting bruises on my elbows or the bony parts of my pelvis as they hit the floor.

"Rolling might hurt a little, but here's your first lesson: good art involves pain."

Gregg's voice was somewhere in front of me, but I couldn't tell if he'd be able to see my eyes if I opened them. I was dying to sneak a peek at Sam, for a good eye roll.

"Now, I want you to hum," Gregg said.

A low vibration of voices began in unison over the sound of rolling bodies.

"Gradually, very gradually, I want you to hum louder."

We did.

"And louder and louder. Now open your mouths and say Aaahhhh."

Were we at the doctor's office?

"More volume!" Gregg shouted. "More! More! Keep rolling! Roll and roll! Back and forth! Don't worry about rolling into each other, on top of each other! Keep your eyes closed!"

I opened mine just as I was rolling toward Sam. Everyone was rolling into each other and screaming and doing everything that Gregg wanted. And their eyes were closed. Except Sam's. I rolled my eyes at him and he rolled his back.

"Eyes shut! No cheating!" Gregg commanded.

Sam shut his and I did too.

We banged into each other. I rolled away, then back toward him again. When I was on my back, Sam tried to roll all the way over me, but he hadn't built up enough momentum. He only made it halfway.

"Sorry. I didn't mean for that to be so weird," he said as he rolled back in the direction he came from.

I wondered what made Sam so awkward. Maybe more physical contact would loosen him up.

"I want you to scream until your throats hurt, till you can feel the rage!" Gregg yelled.

What rage? The rage of being forced to roll on a dirty floor with a bunch of strangers?

I opened my mouth, but no sound came out.

New Views

Sam and I sat with Ralph in the dining hall. I took the seat beside Ralph.

"You guys get to be in the same class?" he asked. "No fair. They shouldn't have split up the Gilloggley Three."

"You're not missing out," I said. "This is going to be a long semester."

"I think it'll be fun," Sam said. "I heard Gregg telling some guy we were gonna use video." He craned his neck around to look behind him. His sterno-cleido-mastoid muscle stretched, forming a line from the back of his ear to his sternal notch.

"It sounds like bullshit to me," I said. "He's not gonna teach us any skills. Except how to freak out."

"I don't know." Sam turned his head in the opposite direction. "Maybe you're right. But I still think it'll be fun."

"I think you'll change your mind," I said.

"Sam," Ralph interjected, "what are you looking for?"

"There's someone I met over break. I thought they'd join us for lunch." He looked around again.

The pit of his neck was deep. I could probably fit two fingertips on its ledge.

"My class isn't so great, either," Ralph said. "The teacher's having us draw a still life, but with our eyes closed and using the hand we don't normally draw with."

"What did the drawings look like?" I asked.

"Just what you'd expect," he said. "Not much. Our teacher says she wants us to have new views of art."

"How can you have a new view with your eyes closed?" I asked.

Ralph laughed. "I should ask."

As I crossed my legs, my foot brushed against Sam's steel-pipe shin.

He gave me this terrified, breath-holding look.

I recrossed my legs in the other direction, this time making sure my foot touched him.

Same reaction.

Don't tell me you have a crush on Sam Slant, I thought. This cannot be happening.

Reason to Talk

The next night, Nate called.

"So how's the beginning of real school?" he asked. There was a banging sound in the background, but different from the radiator. "Glad to be through with Gilloggley?"

"No, I wish I had him back," I said. "I've got this new guy, Gregg Cramroy. Performance Art King."

Nate groaned. The banging was loud and steady. It sounded like he was hammering nails into something.

"So what's up?" I asked.

"Do I need a reason to call?"

"Well, I think so," I said. "Things are different now."

"What do you mean things are different?"

There was a pause, then more banging. I guessed that he'd started on a new nail.

"You know," I said. "We never really worked stuff out after that night."

"What night?"

"You know," I said. "Valentine's night."

"Ellie, aren't you over that by now?" he asked. "I hate games like this. And anyway, I actually do have something important I want to talk to you about."

"So say it."

There was a sudden clunk. Then silence.

"Nate?"

"Sorry." He was back. "I dropped the phone."

"I figured. But what did you want to say?"

"Can I come over?"

"Tell me on the phone."

"But the phone is so impersonal."

"Just tell me on the phone."

"Okay, Ms. Friendly," he said. "I wanted to talk to you about my mom."

"Yeah?"

"I'm all freaked out about her wedding."

"That makes sense," I said. "But you've got to get used to the idea that she's moving on."

"I can't!"

The banging resumed.

"Nate, I can't stand it anymore. What's going on over there?"

"Oh, you mean the noise?"

"Yes. I mean the noise."

"I'm just hanging paintings. I had a few empty spaces to fill up."

"Are they the Sloane paintings?"

"Yeah. They're the only paintings I have here."

"You're calling me for advice while hanging your *Sloane* paintings?"

"Yes. And you don't seem to be giving me any advice."

"I don't know what to tell you," I said quietly.

"What's wrong, Ellie?" he asked. "You're acting so distant. You usually help me through stuff."

"I don't think I can anymore."

"Why not? We can't work this out if you won't tell me why you're upset."

"I used to feel really close to you," I said. "I used to feel like we were perfect for each other."

"Maybe we will be, when we're older."

"I'm not waiting around while you figure out what you want from all the other girls."

"I thought you understood the way things are between me and Clarissa."

"What about Sloane?"

"Look, that's not something to worry about."

"Why not?"

"Because. It's just not."

"That's not gonna do it, Nate. You have to tell me why."

"Fine, I'll tell you everything. But remember, you asked for it."

"Thanks," I said. "I'll try to remember that."

"The last day of class, during the final crit, Sloane announced to everyone that it was a tough decision to take the risk of posing for these paintings. But she said it was worth it because I'm such a gifted painter. Plus, I always made her feel like the most beautiful girl in the world. I couldn't argue with her and say she was lying. Then I'd lose all my credibility. Fritz clapped and said 'Bravo!' with a big smirk."

Pause.

"Are you listening?"

"Yeah."

"So anyway, my class went out for drinks before the party. We get totally sloshed real fast. I mean record time. Then we all go to the party and Sloane gets this idea. She says that she's gonna draw hearts on all the girls' nipples with her lipstick. A few of them are so drunk, they go for it. Then she drags me to the corner and asks me to draw her hearts for her. You know, it would be impossible to draw them upside down on herself, especially when she was drunk, she said. So I did it. I'll tell you, that girl wanted me bad. Real bad. I had a hard time resisting her."

"Did you?"

"Depends on what you mean by resist," he said in a cocky tone that made me want to punch him.

"I don't think I want to know what *you* mean by it."

"Well, I'll tell you, we didn't go all the way."

"Great. That makes me feel better." My voice was flat.

"It should. Because I could've," he said. "But anyway, the thing that sucks is she got an A and I got a B."

"Were her paintings good?" At this point I was talking just to make conversation, not to get information.

"No!" he wailed. "They were so primitive and pasty looking!"

"Do you think Fritz knew?"

"He must have."

"How do you think he found out?"

"I think Maura Bustier told him."

"Why?"

"I think she was jealous that I only painted one of her."

I let out a brief laugh. A mocking laugh.

"It's not funny."

"It sort of is."

"I obviously can't talk to you about anything serious."

"I guess not."

After we hung up my fake smile faded and I lay down flat on my stomach. I pounded the mattress with my fists and my feet like a bad swimmer. And I buried my face in my pillow to muffle my scream.

Art in a Vault

Friday, Gregg treated us to a field trip.

Only about half the class showed up on any given day, because of Gregg's nonattendance policy. And it was never the same people. But it seemed like everyone came for the field trip.

Gregg marched us up to the admissions building, where Ryan Brakee was exhibiting again.

"This guy's a genius, as far as I'm concerned," Gregg announced on our way up the hill. That day he was wearing John-Lennon-style frames. He seemed to have a different pair of glasses for every day of the week.

Sam put his heavy hand on my shoulder. "Try not to barf," he whispered.

The door to the admissions gallery was labeled Brakee: A One-Man Show. The room was empty except for a cubed metal vault in the center of the room. There were small windows on two sides of the cube. We had to take turns peeking through the glass. Inside, the walls were white. Ryan was crouching, gaping at us. There was just enough room for him to stand and to walk about five paces in every direction.

Gregg circled the cell and the tattooed students followed him. His stubble made a scratchy sound as he rubbed it thoughtfully with his fingers.

"One month," he said. "How many of us would have the balls to lock ourselves up for a month?"

The groupies shook their heads.

"I wish," mumbled the guy with the blue mohawk.

"I'd like to lock Gregg up for a month," I whispered to Sam. My lips were really close to his ear.

I took another peek.

A guy dressed in black came in and walked briskly over to the vault with a rattling garbage bag. He kneeled and unlocked a trap door at the bottom of one of the walls. Out of the bag he pulled a shining bedpan and a tray of cafeteria food and he slid them through the slot. Then he locked it back up and left.

Ryan pretended not to notice.

Gregg was watching the scene from the window opposite mine.

Ryan picked up a pencil that lay on the ground and crawled animalistically toward a wall. There he scrawled SCHOOL SUCKS!

"Here we have it!" Gregg cheered. "True art."

As much as I disagreed with that statement, I do have to say, Ryan had come up with a pretty good trick for getting out of doing homework for a month.

Blast from the Past

Since Gregg didn't believe in homework, I made up my own assignments. Over the weekend I drew a self-portrait, using a mirror in my room. I wanted a critique, but I didn't want to bring it to Gregg. So on Monday, a half-hour before class began, I found Ed.

I had looked up his classroom on the schedule. He was in the Garage again. None of his students were there yet when I walked in with my drawing rolled up.

"Ellie!" he shouted. "What a blast from the past! This is just like old times, when you used to walk in that very door!"

"Hi Ed," I said. "I've missed you."

"Oh, no need to flatter me!" he yelled. "How's your new class?"

"Well," I sighed, walking closer, "it's not what I'd expected when I came here. Rolling on the floor and screaming."

Ed stopped beaming.

"One of those," he said.

"Yeah."

"The administration thinks we need more variety in our faculty," he said. "But to me it seems like variety in quality."

"It's just not for me," I said. "Maybe a few years ago it would've been. But not now."

"Are you doing any work outside of class?"

"That's why I came to see you," I said. "I was wondering if you'd still give me critiques even though I'm not your student."

He brightened up again.

"Certainly! Certainly! I'd be delighted!" he shouted. "What've you got here?!"

He pointed at the roll.

"It's a self-portrait." I unrolled it.

"It sure is!" he said. "A lot of emotion too! A brooding expression on that face!"

"Really?"

"Yes," he said. "Self-portraits are very telling."

"I know you don't have time right now to talk," I said. "But I was wondering if you could give me assignments so I don't forget how to draw this semester."

"Sure I will!" he yelled. "What do you want to draw?"

"The figure," I said. "But the problem is I can't afford to hire a model on my own and I don't want to ask my dad for money for this."

"Well, you know, Ellie," Ed said, "the best model anyone can use is free. And I think you've already found her."

"You mean me?"

He nodded vigorously.

"But even for nudes?"

"Only if you're comfortable with that," he said. "You can do it for practice, and just show me ones with clothes. Whatever you want, I'd be happy to help."

"I'll think about it."

"Why don't you bring me a drawing in two weeks and we'll talk!" he shouted. "Here's my number!" He jotted it down on a piece of paper from his shirt pocket. "Call me and we'll set up a time!"

"I will."

"My students will be here soon. I'd better get my act together!"

"Okay," I said. "Thanks for your help."

"Anytime, Ellie! Anytime!"

He waved good-bye with both hands as I left.

Self Reflections

Instead of going to Gregg's class, I went home and pulled the shades.

I got out a big piece of paper, about half my size, and taped it to a board on my easel. Then I sat on the edge of my desk in front of the mirror.

I started to draw myself, just sitting there.

I drew right through lunch. But in the middle of the afternoon I quit. It just wasn't as interesting as Ed's drawings. It wasn't "revealing," like he said self-portraits usually are. Plus, there were so many folds in my sweater and jeans and they kept moving. I couldn't get them right.

I took off my clothes. Not all of them at first. I left on my bra and underwear. But when I started drawing them in, I looked like a Victoria's Secret ad.

I sat there, entirely naked, in front of a blank sheet of paper. I needed a good pose. I tried shifting my legs, my arms, my head. Finally I settled on one foot up on the desk, with the other leg relaxed. My head rested on the raised knee and my hands held that foot. My hair fell over my face.

I sometimes had to draw with my left hand so I could see what my right hand looked like. I had to take breaks to keep my limbs from going dead. And it was really hard to draw my head and at the same time hold it in the right position. But Ed was right; I was a more reliable model than anyone I could've hired. Plus there was no one around to distract me, which was more relaxing than being in a class.

I had a good feeling about this drawing, so I decided to take it slow. I got the basic shapes roughed in, and set it aside for the next day.

Paintings and Pasties

The seniors in the painting department were putting on a show. I was a little worried that the work would be so intimidating I'd be afraid to start painting again.

When I showed up, the room was packed. People in clear plastic jumpsuits were serving hors d'oeuvres. Some of the girls wore pasties and G-strings, but mostly they were all naked underneath the plastic.

A voice behind me said, "I hear that guy over there is a student's father!"

I turned around. Ralph was pointing at a naked guy with a beer gut in one of the plastic suits. Well, he was naked, but he looked like he was wearing a hair suit under the plastic. Curly gray hair covered his body — except his head, which was bald. He had a beard, but he'd shaved his neck all the way down to his collar line. He was handing out pigs-in-blankets.

"Ralph!" I said. "What's going on here?"

"One of the apparel seniors made the outfits. Not very creative, are they?"

"They're no papier-mâché tree."

"I'm telling you, Ellie, you and I could make a whole line of apparel based on wearing your insides on the outside. I've been thinking about this ever since that Valentine's party. I can see the label now: Insides Out. We could even have the seams showing, like they were sewn on the wrong side. It would be way more interesting than this amateur plastic stuff." He gestured at the hors d'oeuvres servers. "I mean, the only thing these outfits say is: Hey, look at me! I'm naked . . . but not really!"

A girl with flower-shaped pasties walked over and offered us some mini-quiches.

We each took one.

"It would be better if they'd painted the pasties to look like real nipples," Ralph whispered.

"Right," I said, laughing. "Have you looked around yet?"

"Yeah." He shrugged. "Pretty disappointing. I'll walk with you."

The first painting was of a dragon getting its head cut off, breathing its last breath of fire in a knight's face. The next one was a white wall with a bloody handprint. It wasn't even painted well. Another was a huge self-portrait with a tear the size of a telephone dripping from the eye. There were only two naturalistic figure paintings. They hung side by side in the darkest corner of the room. Nate's work was way better than both of them.

"Ooh, look at those titles," I said.

"In a Pensive Mood," Ralph read, "and *Melancholy Maiden*." He opened his mouth and stuck his finger inside, pretending to make himself throw up.

"Tell me about it." I laughed.

"What are your paintings like, Ellie?"

"They used to be like this," I said, gesturing to the paintings that surrounded us.

"I can't imagine that."

"Good," I said. "I haven't painted since the end of high school. But I think I want my paintings to look like Ed's drawings."

"Wow," he said. "I liked those. I can't wait to see your paintings. Let me know when you're ready to show them. Maybe I'll design an outfit for your opening. We could print one of your paintings on fabric and make it into a dress, so it looks like you're the figure in the painting."

"Ralph," I said, "the way things are going now, I probably *will* be the figure in the painting."

Old Farts

I stopped going to Gregg's class regularly. Once I showed up after not having gone in for a week and Gregg didn't say anything about it. That day he had us sitting on the floor in a circle talking about what we do to make art a part of our daily lives. He was taping our answers with a video camera.

"You start," he said, aiming the camera at me.

Maybe this was his way of acknowledging my absence.

"I've been drawing every day."

"And?"

"And that's it."

"What do we say to that, class?"

Everyone put their hands to their faces and made farting noises. Blue mohawk guy made armpit farts. I guess it was a trick Gregg had taught them while I'd been away. The only one not doing it was Sam.

"Any other old farts here?" Gregg asked, scanning the ring of farters with his lens. "Hang on. Hang on a second." He put the camera on the floor between him and the guy with the blue mohawk. "These damn things are in the way. I can't focus." He removed his thick round tortoiseshell glasses and put them beside the camera.

"Hey, do you want me to film?" asked blue mohawk guy. "I'm a film major."

"No, I can handle it," Gregg snapped as he lifted the camera to his face.

"Oh, that's cool," said blue mohawk guy. "I didn't mean to imply you couldn't handle it or anything."

"Now where were we?" Gregg asked, aiming the camera at us once again.

Blue mohawk was fidgeting with Gregg's glasses. He squinted at them through his own wiry frames.

"Who will we land on this time?" Gregg turned slowly, surveying his students.

Blue mohawk took off his glasses and delicately placed Gregg's frames over the bridge of his bony nose. He looked confused. "Do you even have a prescription for these things?" he asked.

"Well, not a prescription exactly," Gregg said with a nervous laugh. He held the camera away from his face. "My glasses are what I like to call 'Cosmetoptics,' if you get my drift."

"Yeah. Cosmetic. Optical. I get it." Blue mohawk traded Gregg's glasses back for his own.

"Now," Gregg said looking through the camera, "back to business! Who's next?" He landed on Sam, whose hands were in his lap.

"Over Wintersession I ate every Dunkin' Donuts flavor," Sam confessed.

"Give me more!" Gregg shouted.

"Every doughnut, muffin, and bagel. I tried them each once. Except Boston cream, which I got a few times."

"Where's the passion?" Gregg asked. "It's not art without passion!"

"I needed to know!" Sam's voice rose. "I needed to know what they all tasted like!" He stood up. Gregg followed him with the camera. Sam ran to the corner of the room, where he'd left his backpack. He pulled out his sketchbook and rifled through the pages. Gregg was right behind him. Sam found the page with the doughnuts list. "I wrote it all down, every flavor I bought, so I wouldn't repeat myself!" He waved the book in the air. "But I *had* to repeat myself! I did it for a girl! Because Boston cream was her favorite flavor! I bought it three times!" He didn't look at me once.

"What do we say, class? Is this guy living art?" Gregg asked the circle of students.

The class cheered.

"Yes, I think so," Gregg said. "He saved himself at the end there."

Kind of Guts

"*Had* to do it?" I whispered in the hall after class. "I never asked you to keep buying that flavor. I didn't know it was an art project."

"Neither did I," he said. "But Gregg made me realize that's what it was."

"Do you really believe that?"

"I'm trying to learn what Gregg has to offer," he said. "But he shouldn't have been so mean to you."

"It's all right. I can take it. I've been showing my work to Ed these days. I don't need Gregg."

"Can I see what you've been working on?"

"Sure," I said. "Why don't you walk home with me. And this time you don't have to stand around in the bathroom."

"Okay." He laughed nervously.

"I think about that sometimes," I said as we sploshed through the slush. "I shouldn't have made you wait in there. You could've stood in the same room as me and just turned around. Even if you'd seen me, it wouldn't have been so bad. We see naked people all the time, right?"

"That's true," he said. "I just didn't want to make you uncomfortable."

"Maybe I should warn you," I said, as he wiped his feet repeatedly on my doormat, "you might find my new drawing surprising."

Inside, he immediately spotted the drawing leaning against the wall in the corner of the room.

"Is that you?" he asked.

"It is."

"Man, Ellie," he said. "That's totally rad."

"Thanks."

"No, really," he said. "That takes way more guts than anything Ryan Brakee does. He has the kind of guts it takes to perform onstage, but you have the kind of guts it takes to —" he walked over to the drawing. "The kind of guts it takes to bare your soul."

It was the best compliment anyone could have given me.

Needed

I hadn't checked my e-mail since I'd started my new drawing project. In fact, I hadn't been doing anything much aside from drawing, eating, and sleeping. Whenever I felt lonely or sad, I picked up my charcoal or a book. But one night after dinner I went to the computer lab to see if I had any messages.

There was one. It was from Nate.

> e
> i NEED you. please call me.
> i'm sorry you think i suck.
> n

It was dated three days ago.
I signed off.

You Must Choose

That evening I was supposed to meet with Ed. His night class ended at nine-thirty. This one was in the Garage, too. Ed shouted good wishes at his students as they filed out the door.

"Have a good week, Charlie!"

"Good luck on your homework, Lisa!"

"You're all showing incredible improvement!"

The students shot awkward smiles back at Ed. That must've been what we looked like in the first weeks of our Ed experience.

Ed jumped when I walked in the door.

"Ellie! So glad you came tonight! I've been looking forward to this ever since you came to visit me two weeks ago. Can't wait to see what you've got!"

He hurried me over to the modeling stand, where I unrolled my drawing and laid it down for him to see.

His jaw dropped. Literally.

Squeaky beginnings of words tried to make their way out of his mouth.

"Ellie, I'm speechless," he said. "You've learned a lot since you drew from the figure in my class." His voice was quiet.

My face was hot.

"I've been studying a little," I said.

"You've come a long way!" he shouted. "And you used yourself as a model. Great practice! This isn't just drawn well technically. It's moving. There's a sense of inner struggle."

Then Ed did something he never did when I was in his class; he gave me some real in-depth criticism.

"Keep in mind, Ellie, each part of the body is like those blocks you drew back in the beginning of my class. The head is a sphere, the limbs are cylinders, the torso and pelvis are rectangular solids. You're making these shapes too complex. You're breaking each shape down into thousands of shapes. Think simple."

He drew me some diagrams of how to simplify the figure.

"And toes!" he exclaimed. "Toes have structure! Toes are not worms that dangle off the end of your foot! Make your toes look solid, like you could put weight on them when you walk!"

He bounced up and down on his toes.

"Even tiny components to the body are geometric! They have volume!"

He sketched some feet, with volumetric toes, on the side of my drawing.

"You really want to figure out this anatomy, don't you?"

"Yes."

"Here's what I want you to do," he said. "For next time, Ellie, I want you to redraw this the way I showed you, breaking it down into geometrics, as if the body were made of blocks! Then I want you to make an overlay with tracing paper and I want you to try to draw the skeleton in that pose. Keep it simple! Lines only!"

He was grinning madly.

"Doesn't that sound like fun, Ellie?"

I nodded; it actually did.

"Ellie," he said, "it's not always fun. Drawing the figure is one of the hardest things to do well. You have to make decisions at all times!"

"What do you mean?"

"There are choices every artist must make! Every mark or movement we make is a decision, whether you are performing, abstracting, or creating realistic images. If you fail to consider each decision carefully, your work will be flawed, and it will undermine the emotion you're trying to portray. It's easy to get away with fudging an abstract piece, or even a still life. With the human figure, though, it is agonizingly difficult, because people know what people look like! Here, look at this!" He pointed at the drawing on top of a pile his students had left on the modeling stand. "What's wrong with this torso?"

"The external obliques," I said. "They're too squiggly."

"That's right!" he said. "All muscles are convex! And here it looks like the external obliques are collapsing in on themselves!"

"Looks painful."

"You see? You'll never be able to look at this drawing again, without those obliques bothering you! Even someone who doesn't know anything about anatomy will be stuck on those obliques! They might not be able to tell you exactly what the problem is, but they'll know something is just a little bit off. And then they'll think about that more than they'll think about what the picture is supposed to mean. Understand?"

"I think I do," I said. It was the longest I'd seen him stand in one place, talking calmly. Well, calmly for Ed. This must be what he's like when he's drawing, I thought.

"Most students don't understand this stuff," he said. "I think they could, but I've found that usually, they only want to know the basics. So that's what I give them. But incessant decision-making — that's what separates the pros from the amateurs."

"Are you saying that people who do things like lock themselves in a vault aren't really artists?" I asked.

"Let me put it this way," Ed said. "Art is not all about doing. If that were true, everything would be art." He got on the modeling stand, kneeled, and slowly raised his body into a headstand. "You see?" he shouted, upside down. His face started turning red. "Some people would say, because what I just did was unexpected and wacky, it's art! But let's face it, that would mean I make art about fifty times a day! I don't think I have the energy to be making that much art!" He pedaled his legs in the air as if he were riding a bicycle.

I laughed. If Ed didn't have that much energy, who did?

"Art is about thinking so hard, you're afraid your brain might burst out of your skull! It's about knowing how to control your craft to perfection!" He lowered his legs and turned right side up. He stood, beaming and purple-faced, comb-over flopped to the wrong side of his head. "Ellie, you have the skill to pull off paintings that are just about doing. But I have a feeling you'll be more fulfilled if your work is also about thinking! The choice is yours!" he shouted. "And you must choose!"

Blackout

When I got home that night there was a body sprawled on my doorstep.

His hand was drooped over his face and he was passed out.

Probably some townee high school kid or a homeless guy. Strange, though, that he'd choose to lie on my steps rather than a doorway on Main Street. Maybe I should call a homeless shelter, I thought. The temperature was above freezing, but still it wasn't an ideal night to sleep outside.

The street-lamp bulb in front of my house was burnt out, so I could just barely see his slumped shape.

I immediately headed for the back door so he wouldn't wake up and harass me.

Before I made it around the side of the building, I crept back to take another peek at the guy. There was something familiar about him.

I gasped.

The thick hair — now not quite so electric.

He'd been waiting for me.

I sat on the steps beside him. He reeked of alcohol.

I put my hand on his head.

He didn't budge.

I stroked his hair a few times.

"Nate?" I whispered.

The only movement coming from his body was his breathing.

I wrapped my arms around him and rested my head on his back. I thought about taking him inside, putting him in my bed, and holding him all night.

I wanted to do it without waking him up. But he was too heavy to carry.

I went inside and got a wool blanket. I wrapped it around his entire body, leaving a small opening for his nose and mouth.

In the morning the blanket lay in a heap on my doorstep.

Totally Symbolic

Tchaikovsky's violin concerto was on loud. I was humming along.

I thought the knocking was part of the music. But then I saw Sam through the window, walking away.

I ran to the door. "Hey, come back!" I called.

"I just came by to see what you've been up to," he said as he walked up the steps. "I haven't seen you in class for two weeks."

"I've been drawing at home," I said. "And drawing at the nature lab. And drawing at the library."

I let him in. He closed the door behind him, and stayed facing the door.

He said something I couldn't hear, but I could tell it was a question from his intonation. His voice was so deep, it didn't carry over the music.

"Hang on," I said, turning down Tchaikovsky.

Sam's face was still fixed on the door.

"I said, Do you mind if I look?"

"No, go ahead!" I said. "You didn't have to stay turned around like that!"

"I don't know," he mumbled. "I thought you might want to keep it private."

He walked over to my easel.

The mirror was still leaning against the wall. Beside the mirror, I'd hung the old drawing, which I'd fixed up a bit since my talk with Ed. Books, photocopies, and sketches were splayed all over a table beside the easel.

"Whoa! Check it out!" Sam said.

"I'm still working on it," I said. "I'm having trouble with the ribs. It's hard keeping track of which line belongs to which rib."

"Ribs are your specialty," he said, smiling.

He looked heavy, with his bulky coat and overstuffed backpack.

I took a seat on my bed.

He kept standing.

"Hey, can I have some water?" he asked.

"Help yourself," I said. "But first take off your bag and jacket."

He took off the backpack and laid it by the door. The coat he hung neatly on a chair. Then he went to the kitchen. I heard him opening cupboards, in search of a glass.

Just before I could tell him where to look, he said, "You keep poison on your spice rack?"

I laughed.

"It doesn't look like poison," he said.

"What, you're a poison expert?"

He walked toward me, holding the jar. "No, but I'm a different kind of expert. And I suspect this falls under my area of expertise."

"You sure?"

He opened the jar and smelled it. "Oh, yeah. I'm sure. But what are you doing with this? I thought you weren't a fan."

"I'm not," I said. "Someone gave it to me."

"Are you for real?"

"Unfortunately, yes. You can have it, if you want," I said. "I hear it's good stuff."

His eyes brightened as he lifted his cap from his eyes. "Really?"

"Yeah."

"Whoa, thanks," he said, standing stiffly before me. "I should do something to repay you."

I gestured for him to sit beside me on the bed.

He sat, leaving a two-inch space between us.

I scooted over and closed the gap.

I was about to put my hand on his back, when the side of his leg, his vastus lateralis, tightened and he backed away.

"We can't do this, Ellie."

"Do what?"

He kicked at a knot in the floor.

"You know," he said.

"What are you saying?"

He unscrewed the jar lid, then twisted it back in place.

"I think," he began, then took a deep breath. "I think you're flirting with me. And it's not that I don't like it. I do. It's just I wish you'd done this earlier."

"What are you talking about?" I scooted back a few inches.

He untwisted the jar lid again.

"Look, Ellie. I had a huge crush on you over Wintersession. You knew it. And you know I know you knew it. So don't play dumb. But I gave up because I thought you didn't want to . . . you know . . ."

"What?"

"Go out, or whatever."

"But I was dating someone."

"Yeah, him. As if that mattered. You could've left him so easily."

"Let's not get into that. What about now?"

"Well, now I'm seeing someone. I met her over break and we really hit it off."

"You don't have to sound so apologetic," I said. "I don't really know what I was thinking, anyway." I took a deep breath and exhaled out loud. "This is all pretty embarrassing."

After a long silence, he looked at me and pulled his cap upwards.

"Don't be embarrassed," he said. "I'm just glad you're not still with that Nate guy. You aren't, are you?"

"No." I coiled up and hugged my knee. "I'm not. Sometimes I wish I was. But I know it wouldn't be right."

"Oh my God," he said. "Ellie, you're in exactly the same position as your drawing. That's got to be totally symbolic or something!"

Completely Platonic Coffee

"Long time no see," Nate said. His hair had grown out and sat tamely on his head.

I suddenly felt like shriveling up into a little ball and rolling away. I hadn't noticed him coming toward me down the hill, and I wasn't prepared to talk to him.

"Hey," I said.

"How are things?"

"Fine," I said. "But I wish spring would get here already."

"Do you want to hang out sometime?" he asked, touching my elbow.

"I'm really busy these days."

"No, I mean just as friends. I swear."

Maybe it wouldn't be so bad if we just sat down and talked in some neutral place. Maybe what we really needed was to talk.

"We'll go for coffee," he said. "Completely platonic."

"How about now?" I wanted to do it before I changed my mind.

We went to True Brew on Main Street. And as we sat, I realized there was nothing to say. There was nothing to say as friends because we never had been friends. Right from the start we were lovers. The Devil and a gypsy.

"Hey, do you know who Elvis was?" I asked.

"Elvis? What do you mean? Everybody's heard of Elvis."

"No, the guy dressed as Elvis! At the Artist's Ball."

"I don't know," he said. "Some guy."

His hand was rumbling on the table and his knees wouldn't stay still.

"Why won't you answer my messages?" he asked.

"Because it's not right," I said. "We're not right. You have a girlfriend."

"But I told you, we have —"

He started swishing his coffee cup. Round and round.

"I know, an open relationship. I can't be a part of it."

"Well, if we never talk to each other again, it'll be all your fault," he said. "I'm trying."

I was about to disagree but before I could, the coffee slipped out of Nate's grasp and skidded to the edge of the table, where it finally fell on his lap.

"Shit!" he yelled. When he stood up, it looked like he'd peed in his pants. "Shit, shit!" he yelled again, and ran to the bathroom.

I grabbed a pile of napkins and brought them to the table. Coffee rivers were dribbling from under our table to the surrounding tables. A J. Crew modelly–looking woman snatched her suede purse from the floor to keep it from getting wet. A guy in a striped tie lifted what looked like a laptop.

I'd need another pile of napkins to clean it all up.

I started walking to the counter to get more, but instead of stopping when I got there, I walked right out the door. By the time I got to the corner I was running.

My quadriceps and hamstrings contracted and relaxed as fast as they could. I hadn't run in a while. I wished it was dark out, and nobody else was on the streets watching me run.

I remembered how exciting it used to feel, running home from Nate's at night. It's funny: I'd mistaken that exhilaration for independence, for a sense of confidence in a situation beyond my control. I would run there with the feeling that of all the girls in Nate's life, he liked me best. And I'd run home, trying to hold on to as much of that feeling as I could. But if Nate had really felt that way about me, I wouldn't have needed to run.

When I turned onto Artist's Row I was already winded. I kept going anyway.

And I ran all the way home without looking back.

Going Twice

A few days later I got an e-mail from Nate:

> i'm not sure what's going on with you but you won't
> LISTEN to me so i'm writing and i hope you'll read
> this all the way through. i really feel like we're hon-

estly HONESTLY soul mates. i feel like we could work things out. the only thing that's wrecking this is YOU. maybe you don't realize how good we are for each other because you're so inexperienced. i've been with a lot of girls, like i told you, and it doesn't get any better than it was with you. what about our father connection? how can you just give that up? we NEED each other. i need you to help GET ME THROUGH my mom's wedding. nobody else can comfort me right now.

and i hope hope hope this isn't about stupid sloane. remember, YOU were in on the joke. SHE wasn't.

that's all from me until you CARE. going once, going twice . . .

I didn't write back.

I had a feeling "GET ME THROUGH my mom's wedding" meant "GET ME SOME sex because nobody will give it to me this week."

The weird thing is, part of his note seemed right. Part of me felt like I still needed him. But I wasn't sure it was him exactly that I needed.

There was something he had dead wrong, though. One of us did know our dad.

Or at least knew enough.

Escape

Halfway through the semester, Gregg gave us midterm evaluations. We had to sign up for times to meet with him individually. We were supposed to prepare something outside of class to show him.

Blue mohawk guy was waiting outside the door to the classroom when I showed up for my time. Gregg was running a little behind schedule. I had brought my drawings for Ed with me, since I had nothing else to show.

Blue mohawk was carrying a plastic wastebasket.

"What's that for?" I asked him.

"I can puke on command," he said, grinning. "Gregg's gonna love it."

"I bet he will."

That was a talent I sometimes wished I had in Gregg's class.

In a few minutes, the door opened and Sam came out.

Blue mohawk entered the room.

"You next?" Sam asked.

"Yeah."

"Are those your drawings for Ed?"

"They are."

"Man, good luck," he said. "I was jumping around like a monkey and making ape noises, just because I thought he'd like it. But he said I was faking, and that I didn't really want to be acting like a monkey. Which I guess is right, but I thought it would get me a good grade."

"What a jerk," I said. "Are you going anywhere now?"

"I'm meeting someone for dinner," he said. "Why?"

"Do you want to hang out until dinner? You could stick around and wait for me."

"Sure."

When blue mohawk exited the room, he had a gleam in his eye. The wastebasket was empty.

The place stank when I walked in.

A puddle of vomit lay beneath Gregg's swinging legs. Stray specks were spattered on his shoes.

"He missed the bucket," Gregg said. His mini oval glasses barely had frames. The lenses looked like two clear disks floating on his face.

"By a lot," I said.

"What've you got for me? It's gonna be hard to beat the guy who went before you."

I unrolled my drawings.

"You've *got* to be kidding," he said.

"About what?"

"This is exactly the garbage I told you guys I didn't want to see in here."

"What's wrong with it?"

"It's so old school," he said. "There's no way you can do anything that hasn't already been done before."

"What if I don't care?" I challenged. "What if all I want to do is represent real life?"

"Why represent real life when we're surrounded by it? Art should be a way of escaping real life."

His legs swung faster.

"If you tore that drawing up, it would be more of a statement."

"What if I just walked out of this meeting?"

"That —" He laughed. "That's more like it! You've got me there!"

I stormed out, drawings flapping at my side.

What Did It

"What happened?!" Sam asked when he saw me emerge from the room all worked up.

"I think I won him over," I said. "Not on purpose. But I won't fail."

"I've got to hear this," he said. "I'm supposed to meet Hannah in the dining hall in an hour. That should give us more than enough time."

"Is Hannah your girlfriend?"

"Yeah." His ears reddened.

"Let's not talk here," I said. "I want to get away from Gregg and his fan club."

It was almost completely dark outside. Without the sun it was pretty cold. We needed to find a nearby building to pass the time until Sam had to go.

"I've got an idea," I said.

The Garage was completely empty. I'd never seen it with all the lights off. It seemed like dead bodies probably could rise out of those sinks. But once the lights were on, it was the same old Garage.

Sam slouched across from me on a stool as I described my "evaluation" with Gregg.

"Right on," Sam said. "You know, you were right when you said I'd get sick of him."

"Really?"

"Yeah, for the first time I felt like a total idiot in that classroom."

"You never felt like an idiot doing Gregg's dumb assignments?"

"No, man," he said. "Usually it's fun, 'cause there are all these other people jumping around too. You're all in it together, you know? But doing it alone doesn't feel like art. It's just you acting like a weirdo in front of a guy who's judging you."

"That's part of why I can't stand him," I said. "He's so judgmental. I mean, I want my teachers to be hard on me, but his standards are so inconsistent. One minute he cheers you on if you're, let's say, acting like a monkey, and the next minute he accuses you of not feeling it enough."

"Maybe if I'd had a banana I would've seemed more into it. The worst part is, he'll probably fail me for not really wanting to be a monkey."

"I'm sure you won't fail."

"Who knows?" he said. "Maybe if he flunked all of us, he'd think of it as art."

"Maybe," I said. "But he'd probably lose his job."

Sam adjusted his cap and looked at the ceiling.

"Remember that night we were in here and you told me people would never understand me if I kept my thoughts to myself?"

"You were in your chill space."

"Right." He smiled. "That's what did it."

"That's what did what?"

"That's what made me able to talk to Hannah. If I hadn't thought about that stuff you said to me, I wouldn't have opened up to her when she first started talking to me over break."

There was a long silence before I said, "I'm glad to hear that. It's no good to keep everything packed away in your head."

"Yeah," he said. "I think that's what I liked about Gregg's class at first. It gave me the chance to let all my thoughts out. It let me be the loud person I'll never be. But that excitement is wearing off."

"I know what you mean."

Another long silence.

"Hey," he said, unslouching, "do you want to have dinner with me and Hannah?"

"You don't think that would be weird?"

"No way," he said. "Do you?"

"Well, after what happened a few days ago . . ."

"That was nothing," he said. "And it would be my honor to introduce my two favorite NECAD people to each other."

Crunchy Like Me

She was waiting by the dining hall door in her dreadlocks and long tie-dyed dress.

"I brought a friend," Sam said as Hannah hugged him.

The back of Sam's neck muscles seemed to relax.

"Ellie?" she asked when she released him.

I nodded.

"Great to meet you." She smiled and stretched her arms out to hug me, too. She wasn't fat, but her body felt pillowy. With anyone else, I would've felt strange about hugging at our first meeting, but with her it seemed natural. Like this is what she probably did with everybody.

"That's some awesome weed you gave Sam," she said. "I can't believe you just gave it away. Join us anytime if you have second thoughts."

"Thanks," I said, "but I don't think that'll happen."

"I'll save us a booth," she said. "You two get in line. And Sam, let me take that bag for you. The thing looks like it's gonna explode."

He handed his backpack over.

"She's crunchy, like me," Sam whispered to me as we filled our trays.

"Birkenstocks and all," I said.

When we got to the table, Hannah went to get dinner.

"I can't wait to hear about the midterm critiques!" she said, with an emphasis on *critiques* that made me think she knew what Gregg's class was like.

Sam sat on her side of the table and I sat across from him.

"What's her major?" I asked.

"Illustration," he said. "She illustrates kids' books. She's graduating this year and she's already got a deal. Some kind of potty book."

"Like how to go to the potty?"

"Yeah, like that." He raised his cap and turned to watch her at the salad bar. "Hannah's vegan," he said. "Like Ralph. I never thought I'd date a vegan."

I laughed. "I never thought you would either."

He gave me a *What're you gonna do?* shrug. His arms finally looked relaxed when they moved.

When Hannah came back with her big leafy salad, she said, "So tell me about the crits."

Sam and I took turns telling her about our day.

"Right on, Ellie," she said. "Gregg's no teacher. He's a bully. That's what I've been trying to tell this guy all along." She took off Sam's cap and ruffled his flattened dreads.

I'd never seen the top of Sam's head before. It looked smaller without his hat.

"I know, I know," he said, yanking his cap back. "You don't need to convince me anymore."

I spotted the fruit bin. "Hannah, did you know Sam thinks Gregg would've been more impressed with his performance if he'd been jumping around with a banana?"

Hannah let out a hearty laugh. It came out so easily, like she really meant it. "A banana? Sam, tell me she made that up!"

"No," he said sheepishly. "It's true. I think I would've seemed more into it."

"Dude, I'll buy you a banana," Hannah said. "You can try it for us right now. Maybe you'll actually convince us that you want to be a monkey."

Sam shoved her playfully. He rolled his eyes at me.

As I walked home that night, I was glad that nothing had ever happened between me and Sam. He and Hannah were so good together. Plus, I don't think I ever really wanted him.

It's just, it would've been so easy . . .

Stopping By

At times I'd pass Nate's place without the thought of him ever crossing my mind.

But other times I'd see a light on, and I'd be tempted to stop by, just to see. To see what? I'm not sure. Maybe to see if anything had changed. At those times, it was like there was a magnet in my heart. And there was an oppositely charged magnet in his house, trying to drag me through the path from the road. I'd have to cross the street and walk on the other side, just to fight off the tug.

Sometime in spring, I thought I'd see if he was in.

My head was down as I went up the path to the side of his house, thinking of what I'd say to him. "Just wanted to say hi, see how you were doing . . ." Something that would sound friendly, but not too inviting.

I didn't see that someone else had beat me to the door.

Her porn star–type, probably boob-jobbed body was already entering the doorway.

It was too late to go back; he'd seen me.

I didn't move any closer. Neither did he.

And despite everything I was feeling, a smile forced its way across my face. I had been so wrong, trying to fish for opening lines. There was nothing left to say. I turned around, taking with me my obnoxious grin that wouldn't go away.

By the time I got to the street he had let the door slam and I heard his sock-covered feet running toward me down the path. But I kept going.

He stopped at the corner and hissed at my back, "I never slept with her while we were together!"

"And I never thought you did!" I shouted back.

Sarcasm could still come in handy.

In the Shower

At home I showered, water steaming hot. Tchaikovsky's violin concerto seeping through the open door. I was humming along when all of a sudden I wanted to turn the music off. It was working its way into my head. Rushing through my blood. The tears were hot like the spluttering shower. They kept coming and coming, no matter how much I told myself to stop. I bent over and held my face in my hands, body convulsing with every sob.

Somehow I felt I wasn't crying for him exactly. Those tears were for something else. Something else, only partly related to Nate.

When I stopped, it was over. My body felt like I'd been in a fight. It also felt clean. Not just my skin, but my insides too. As if I'd taken an intravenous breath mint.

I turned the knob to cold before getting out.

Something Else

I've done a good job of blocking him out of my memory.

But sometimes late at night when I'm teetering on the brink of sleep or running home through lamp-lit streets, I think of him. And I want nothing more than to feel him beside me.

Not to see or to hear him.

Just to be faintly aware of his breathing while I dream.

Better Than Running at Night

It's the Fourth of July and I'm expected to bring ketchup to my friend's neighborhood barbecue. She wants to set me up with the guy who's bringing the mustard. But the leaves are applauding the first thunderstorm of the summer and I'd rather stay in bed. My windows are open and the cool rain is misting my skin through the screens. The apartment shakes with each kaboom and cars swish through puddles. Nothing could make me want to get up, no matter how late it is. There will be more barbecues, other guys to meet. And they can find ketchup somewhere else, anyway.

I'm wearing a project I'm working on with Ralph. Pajamas — since I told him I wouldn't wear something like this out of my apartment. He sewed stretchy fabric to fit perfectly over my body. I painted the right half to look like bones and I'll paint the left half to look like muscles. Ralph added gloves and booties that hang off the ends of the arm and leg holes. I'll paint those, too.

I reach over to the bookshelf where I keep all my old sketchbooks, and pull out the first one from NECAD. I flip through the pages, stopping on a drawing I did of a fire hydrant morphing into

Clarissa. Looking at her makes me laugh out loud. I haven't thought about her in a while.

I also come across a drawing of a guy in spandex jogging gear running through the rain. I remember seeing him one night while running home. As he approached me, I thought about how strange he looked, racing through raindrops after midnight. Couldn't this have waited until the morning? I wanted to ask him. And it suddenly occurred to me — I was doing the same thing. When the guy passed me, he smiled and called out, "What's better than running at night?" I didn't have an answer then. But now, after everything that happened with Nate, I think maybe I do.

I put my sketchbook on the floor and pull the gloves and booties over my hands and feet. The rain has stopped sounding like individual raindrops, making one continuous TV static gush.

I lie back and shut my eyes. And I hover between waking and dreaming while thunder pelts water at my windowpanes and lightning shatters the sky.